All that could have been

SOON TO BE A MAJOR MOTION PICTURE
hamaari adhuri kahaani

MAHESH BHATT

with Suhrita Sengupta

SPEAKING
TIGER

Mahesh Bhatt is an acclaimed and popular film director, producer and screenwriter. In addition to the landmark films *Arth* (1982), *Saaransh* (1984), *Janam* (1985), *Daddy* (1989), *Awaargi* (1990) and *Zakhm* (1998), his work as director and screenwriter includes commercial hits such as *Aashiqui* (1990), *Dil Hai Ki Manta Nahin* (1991) and *Sadak* (1991). Since he retired as director in 1999, he has written and produced several successful films, among them, *Raaz* (2002), *Jism* (2003) and *Murder* (2004).

Mahesh Bhatt is also the author of two books: *U.G. Krishnamurti: A Life* and *A Taste of Life: The Last Days of U.G. Krishnamurti.*

All that could have been

MAHESH BHATT

with Suhrita Sengupta

All that could have been

SOON TO BE A MAJOR MOTION PICTURE

hamari adhuri kahani

SPEAKING
TIGER

SPEAKING TIGER
An imprint of FEEL Books Pvt. Ltd
4381/4, Ansari Road, Daryaganj
New Delhi 110002

First published in Speaking Tiger as a paperback in 2015

ISBN: 978-9385288241

10 9 8 7 6 5 4 3 2 1

Typeset in Perpetua Regular by SÜRYA, New Delhi

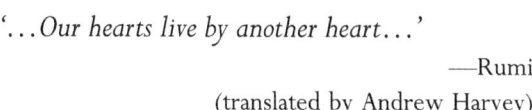

'…*Our hearts live by another heart*…'

—Rumi
(translated by Andrew Harvey)

PROLOGUE

The bus lurches and her head hits the window, bringing her awake with a start. The woman next to her sighs, 'Arre baap re,' and goes back to sleep.

Vasudha watches the elderly woman, not much older than herself. She envies her this ability to shut her eyes and shut out the world. When Vasudha closes her eyes, sleep does not come. She pulls her red sweater close around her and opens the window. The bus fills with the sweet scent of the mahua flower. She doesn't need to look at the crumpled old map in her hand. She's here.

The tears come now. It is as if this smell has all her life in it. It has the India she had lost in those years in Dubai. It has the friends she had left behind—dear sweet Maddy, and Naila.

It has the child who kept her sane.

It has him.

'You live in your nose, don't you?' he had laughed

once. And she had said, 'Don't we all? It's what we smell that we remember most. The smell of school and chalk powder. Kheer bubbling on the fire. Woodsmoke. The sea. These flowers, this garden...' And she had stopped there. She hadn't said the rest: 'This is how we remember, and this is how I remember you. The smell of your breath when we stand close. The scent of your sweat in the desert where you want me to grow you a garden.'

She stands up now and walks unsteadily to the door of the bus.

There's a thin flush of light on the horizon when the bus pulls away on the wide road flanked by mahua trees. She stands by the side of the road, then begins to walk across, slowly, as if trying to remember a long-forgotten route. There's a milestone ahead that reads: Bastar, 3 km.

The air is cool and kind, but it will not hold her. Something tells her that it is time for the long, deep breath that fuses everything she has felt and not felt, what she has done and left undone, what she has seen and imagined. One long, deep breath for sweetness and for farewell.

And then the world spins and she falls, clutching her heart. But she is now a mahua flower and when her body hits the ground it is with no more pain than a leaf falling when autumn calls.

ONE

The man was smiling at her as he drew the needle down her arm. It was a parody of a smile, full of malice and misogyny.

'What shall I write here?' he asked.

She looked at him for a moment and his face swam into focus. It was Anil, the goonda from down the street. How had she got here? How had he managed...? She began to struggle and found that someone was holding down her feet. She raised her head and saw that it was Samson. It would be. They hunted in pairs, the two of them, always hanging around the street when she was on her way to work or taking Saanjh to school.

'Please...' she began and even as she said it she knew how pointless it was to ask them for mercy. But she had to try.

'Please what?'

A third voice. How many were there? The voice had

come from behind her, from her past. It was not a voice she had heard in many years.

'Hari?'

'Indeed. How are you, my queen? Long time no see.'

'Hari...' she moaned. 'Hari.'

'That's me. And you will bear my name. I shall inscribe it on your body and in your heart.'

'I like that,' said Anil with a leer. 'Let's do the heart bit first.'

He leaned down to grab her blouse. She began to scream...

'Maa?'

A voice broke through her nightmare. She woke up to the small room, the haven she had constructed slowly and laboriously for herself and her son.

'Maa?'

Saanjh. She switched on the light. He was standing by her bed, carrying a tumbler full of water. His lower lip was trembling.

'Bad dream again?' he said and offered her the glass.

'Yes,' she said before she could stop herself. Then she took the glass from him and drank it down and reached for him. 'It must be something I ate.'

He nuzzled into her and she drew the cover over him.

'Sleep now,' he said. 'Sleep, Maa. Everything is okay.'

He was comforting her. She felt something move and shift behind her sternum. Her child was comforting her. She thought she might cry so she made her voice mock-stern and said, 'Yes, everything's okay. Sleep. It's a work day for both of us tomorrow.'

'And a big day, too!' he said, his voice suddenly mischievous, suddenly shedding years.

'Yes, I remember.'

'Do you think he'll come tomorrow?'

'Who, my love?'

But he was already asleep, with a child's ability to turn off the lights inside his head. She lay back and tried not to think about her dream. But as she raised her arm to cover her head, the tattoo on the inside of her arm caught her eye. Hari. He had wanted to brand her.

On the first day of their honeymoon, he had taken her to the man who did the tattoos. No tattoo artist this, no parlour for him, just a needle and some ink and a dirty piece of cloth with which to clean it. She had been lucky that she hadn't ended up with some skin disease. He had just finished putting an Om symbol on a young man's hand when Hari dragged her up.

'What will it be?' the tattoo man asked her.

'You don't need to ask her. Ask me,' said Hari.

'Okay, what will it be?' the man said.

'Put my name on her. She's mine. Make it nice and big so everyone knows.'

'Certainly, sir.'

'So get on with it.'

'You'll have to tell me your name, sir, then I can get on with it.'

'Don't act smart. Hari. Write Hari.'

'What about a surname?'

'Hey, I know your kind. Want to make money off me? Hari will do. How many Haris can there be in her life?'

One, she thought now, as she drew the sleeve of her nightgown down to cover the tattoo. One was enough. For a lifetime. With an effort, she closed her eyes. There was work to do, flowers waiting for her. She pushed her nose into her son's hair; the sweet scent of his childhood always reassured her. She fell into a dreamless sleep.

When she awoke, he was still curled up in a ball, his hand tucked against his chin. She resisted the urge to kiss him—this was the sweetest sleep of all, the one before morning came, and she had some things to do. She crept quietly to the dining table and dragged a crate from under it. There was a second-hand computer in it, the best she could afford. She uncovered it and set it on the table and sat down to write a note to go with it.

She began in her usual handwriting and then remembered. She took a fresh sheet of paper and began to write again, carefully disguising her handwriting.

Dear Son,

I'm sorry I can't make it again today. But I know that you are growing big and strong and will take care of your Mama while I am away. I wanted you to have a computer so that you can look at the world through it and understand how different we are from other people and how similar too. I hope you will make good use of it.

Love,

Papa

Her hand trembled as she signed. How long could she go on playing this game? As long as Saanjh needs you to, an inner voice answered her, and there he was next to the table.

'Look what your Papa sent,' she said after she had kissed him.

'Wow, cool!' he said. 'Is it for me?'

'No, it's for the little boy who lives down the lane.'

'Ma! The line is: and none for the little boy who lives down the lane.'

'And it is your birthday, isn't it? So it must be for you?'

A cloud appeared on his smooth brow.

'Papa?'

'Oh darling, he called and wanted to talk to you. But when I told him you were asleep, he said I shouldn't disturb you.'

'Oh Maa.'

'And there's *my* gift for you.'

On the window, a potted plant. It was a periwinkle and as if for the day, it had blossomed with a single white flower.

Saanjh went across dutifully.

'Talk to it,' she said.

'Maa-aa.'

'No, it's scientifically proven that flowers like to be talked to.'

'Because it gives them carbon dioxide, I suppose? Hello, Phool.'

'That's a lovely name.'

'Welcome to the family, Phool. Just me and my Maa but my Papa is coming home soon. So he says. He's always lying to me.'

'Saanjh.'

Her voice had a warning note.

'Phool? Tell her it's my birthday. She can't scold me today.'

'Saanjh.'

He grinned and came back to the computer and settled down. Behind his head, a butterfly fluttered and hovered and then came to rest on Phool. Vasudha offered up a silent prayer: 'May that be an omen for both of us.'

'Now don't take too much time over that computer,' she said. 'We have a bus to catch.'

'And breakfast to eat.'

'It's your day. What do you want?'

'Aaloo parathas,' he said, but his fingers were already dancing over the keyboard. Vasudha took a moment to watch him, to let herself feel a trickle of pride. The words of William Blake, long-forgotten, from the days when poetry still meant something, suddenly surfaced in her mind: *'Joy and woe are woven fine, a clothing for the soul divine. Under every grief and pine, runs a joy with silken twine.'*

She had not wanted to marry Hari. She had tried to dissuade her father but he had been completely adamant. As they walked home together from the market one evening, she had tried to put her side to it. 'Pappa, I don't love this man?'

He stopped and looked at her.

'Love? So this is what studying literature does to you.'

Then he looked around at the houses in the street.

'In how many of these houses do you think the women love their husbands?'

'I don't know...'

'I do. Not one of them. Nothing survives marriage. Not love, not hate. Marriage is like a grinding stone. Everything gets mixed up.'

'Didn't you love...?'

'She left me so young. She left me with you. And I have cared for you and looked after you. I have worried about you for too many years. It's time for someone else to take you on.'

His words were like stones. She looked at him carefully now but he didn't even seem to know that he was hurting her. Perhaps they were words he had heard someone else use and hadn't thought about. Was that all she was: care and worry?

'Pappa, I can look after myself.'

'Can you? Okay, let us say that you can. But a woman alone in our society does not live an easy life. Don't fight tradition, Vasudha. I know the boy, he's a pujari's son, they are Brahmins like us. These things are important. He'll be the right husband for you. A woman needs security, not love.'

His words came back to Vasudha now as she kneaded the flour and popped the pressure cooker open to release the potatoes. Anil and Samson made the daily walk to the bus stop a nightmare. Not just for her but for Saanjh too. He knew that they aimed their sexual barbs at her. He felt that he had to protect her but he didn't know how. How could he? He was only eight years old. But he had a man-sized sense of responsibility. Was that her doing too?

No, Hari had done that to both of them. She would not bear the guilt for crimes that were not hers. She had agreed to marry him against her better wishes, sensing a darkness in him. She had taken the woe that went with it. But then it had brought her the joy that sat now at a computer, fingers flying, eyes shining, the world opening up for him.

She averted her eyes, feeling for a moment the old atavistic fear of casting the evil eye upon her own child.

~

She braced herself at the door, unaware that Saanjh's eyes were on her. Then she set her jaw and plunged into the outside world, her son at her side. In her head she carried an image of the Devi. But the goons were lying in wait on the road and began their serenade of catcalls and lewd comments.

'It's getting cold at night, rani. You need something to warm your thighs?'

'Arrey Samson, you're talking rubbish. How can it be cold when I'm getting hot? And she knows I can warm her nice and long.'

Vasudha caught Saanjh looking at her and she forced a smile. In the distance, she could see a familiar red form. Thank heavens for the BEST and its services. She grabbed Saanjh's arm and said, 'The bus. Let's go.'

And they were running for it.

Seconds later, she breathed a sigh of relief and tried not to look back. Once again, she had eluded them. Once again, her luck had held. But the thought followed: 'How much longer?'

'Got your éclairs?'

'Yes, Maa.'

'Got the Five-Stars for your teachers?'

'Yes, Maa.'

And soon it was time for him to get off.

'See you, Maa.'

'Have a good day.'

'You too, Maa.'

Then he was running into school and the gates were closing behind him and she could breathe a sigh of relief. For a little while, he was in the care and protection of the school and she could focus on the flowers.

~

As she entered the hotel, the flower service man saw her from a distance and gathered up some anthuriums.

'They are good flowers, madam, value for money,' he said when she came up to him. 'Last for a week at least. Take from here, put there. Take from there, put here. No problem.'

'It's the time for rajnigandha, isn't it?'

'Arre, Madam, rajnigandha is old news. Today everyone is looking for foreign flowers. Now anthuriums, Madam, they look like foreign but they grow in Alibag. And Madam, should not say it, but sexy flowers they are.'

There would be no relief from this. 'If you have no tuberoses,' Vasudha said finally, 'I'm going to find someone else.'

'Don't do like that, Madam. I will send. Now only.'

'Thank you very much,' she said icily. And then she turned with relief to the world of flowers. Rajnigandha had the right fragrance for a day like this. It would remind the foreign guests that they were in another country, while everywhere they were cocooned from its realities by an attentive English-speaking staff, laundered carpets, bottled water and air-conditioning. Anthuriums, on the other hand, she used for the Indian guests who threw weddings there and wanted everyone to know that they had paid for the floral arrangements by the stick.

Later, as she walked into the flower depository, she knew she had been right. Rajnigandha would work its magic. She dipped her head to the tightly-rolled buds and drew their fresh green energy into her body.

'And what deep-deep thoughts you're having today?'

Vasudha turned at the familiar voice.

'Good morning, Maddy. I was just thinking of rajnigandhas,' she smiled at her friend.

'Amol Palekar-wali? You know, the other day I was thinking, we all marry Amol Palekars but we dream of Aarav Ruparel.'

'I was actually thinking about the flower, not the film.'

'Ohffho! You toh are like that only. The whole world is making a great hoo-haa over Ruparel coming here and you are thinking of your tubers.'

'Tuberoses. Tubers are potatoes.'

'The potatoes can go buy oil. You know about Aarav Ruparel?'

'I'm sure you're going to tell me.'

Vasudha could see that this was going to take some time so she began her stock-taking.

'Haai. Very saarky you are this morning! But anyway, I am a kind and forgiving soul, what to do? So I will tell you the goss. He has one hundred and eight hotels and no home of his own.'

Vasudha began to count the red roses. What was it about red roses? Why did people love them so much? Because they spoke of love?

'You're listening? I was saying he has no home of his own. He has only Air India ka 001 seat booked in his name, all the time. Can you believe? Multibillionaire like that? If you ask one taxiwala, be tereko kya chaahiye, he's going to say, first house, then car, then whatever-falaana-dhimkana.

But this man who has hotels…Accha if you're not listening I'm going.'

Vasudha turned to her friend with a smile. She was used to Maddy and her threats and her poses. They were all part of the infectious energy and enthusiasm with which she viewed life. There were times when she envied Maddy's uncomplicated attitude but there were others when she recognised that much of it was a disguise.

'I wish I could stay and talk, Maddy, but flowers have their own time.'

'You and your flovverrs. Chalo, I know when I'm not wanted. You brought lunch?'

'Yes. Aaloo parathas.'

'Arre, you made my day. One full paratha?'

'Don't worry, I brought you your share.'

'You're a living doll. No, you're one full guldasta. Mwaah.'

Vasudha turned back to her work with a sigh of relief. Maddy was a wonderful friend but she could be tiring sometimes.

A cough behind her brought her up again, out of the world of the floral arrangement. It was Leena, head of housekeeping.

'No,' Vasudha said.

'What do you mean, 'No'? You haven't even heard me ask something, have you?'

'You're not going to ask, then?'

'Oh come on, babes, would I ask you if I didn't know you were the only one who could handle it?'

'That's what I meant when I said no. I have the Crystal Ball Room to do and then I have to attend to the poolside. Only then…'

'No, Vasudha. This is an emergency.'

It sometimes struck Vasudha that the word 'Emergency' was used rather loosely. An emergency in a hospital? Certainly. An emergency on the floor of a manufacturing company? Possible. An emergency in a bank? Likely enough these days, from what she read in the papers. But what emergency could a hotel have that meant the chief florist was the only one who could help?

'You see, Aarav Ruparel is checking in today.'

That name again.

'Well, he won't be in until noon, right?'

'Darling, when Aarav Ruparel checks in, he doesn't follow the rules of the ordinary guest. He will expect to enter his room when he enters the hotel. His flight should be landing at any moment now,' Leena said, looking at the fake Rolex on her wrist. 'The register will go up to him, he won't come to the counter. And he will notice if his room isn't in tip-top shape. So I want you there. Now. I don't care who's booked the Crystal Ball Room and I don't care who's in the pool. As though those fat old men ever look at the flowers; they're only interested in how many bikinis are in the water.'

Hotel emergencies generally involved the rich and the famous. Rude, arrogant, expecting all the world to be at their service at the snap of their fingers.

'Stop it,' Vasudha told herself, as she made her way to the Presidential Suite. 'This is your job. It gives you your freedom. It feeds and clothes and schools Saanjh and even makes it possible for you to buy him a second-hand computer and put it down to his father's doing. You shouldn't even *think* badly about it.'

And then she got down to work. As usual the flowers worked their magic. When she had finished, she stepped back from them and looked at them. She folded her hands and bowed her head, unaware of the man who had stepped out of the bathroom behind her, dressed in a pair of shorts and a t-shirt.

'Yes, you should have been in a garden somewhere. I know that you should have been the playground of butterflies and that bees should have sucked nectar from you to turn it into honey. I know that you should have felt the wind play with your leaves and the sun caress you and bless you. But we have brought you here to die for us. For this I ask your forgiveness. I can only say that in your gifts, the gift of beauty given to the florist who cuts you from your tree, the gift of perfume given to the hand that crushes you, there is much that we can learn. Thank you and forgive me.'

The sound of clapping broke in on her.

She spun round.

'That was mad but lovely. I've never heard anyone apologise to a flower before.'

Vasudha would remember that moment in a series of flashes. The voice first. Like the rumble of a finely-tuned engine. Those arms that looked like they could shield a woman from the world. That hair, tousled from drying. The legs…no, she hadn't looked at them. She had been taught not to stare…so how come that image was so clearly embedded in her brain?

'I'm sorry,' she said. 'I did knock when I came in.'

'I must have been showering. But…' and here he approached her to peer at her nametag, 'Vasudha. I'm delighted that I didn't hear you knock. Or I wouldn't have heard you talk to those flowers.'

She felt her face blush.

'You're troubled by what you do, aren't you?'

She smiled.

'What is it that you don't like about your job?' he asked suddenly.

'I…' she said, then stopped.

'Come on,' he said. 'I won't tell.'

'I once told my boss that it would make so much sense to have growing plants in hotel rooms. You know, guests would come in and maybe a few of them would notice that there was life in the rooms rather than death.'

'Life rather than death,' the man muttered. He seemed to be testing the idea on his tongue and in his mind.

'I always remember what George Bernard Shaw said about cut flowers. He said, "I like babies too but that doesn't mean I cut off their heads and stick them in vases."'

'Is that how you see them?'

'The guests go away in the morning and that's when my

people come and clear away the bodies. The fallen petals, the blackened roses, the withered leaves. I see this every day. And I wonder: could we not bring more life into being—more flowers, more oxygen, more growth? Must we contribute to death?'

'That's a beautiful idea. Did you share it with this hotel?'

'I did tell Leena about it.'

'Who's Leena?'

'She's the head of housekeeping here.'

'What did she reply?'

'She said that the hotel prides itself on its international standards. That every hotel has cut flowers in the rooms and that we would also, therefore, have cut flowers in our rooms.'

'Wow.'

She looked at him doubtfully and then saw an ormolu clock behind him.

'Is that the time? I have so much to do! Excuse me.'

She picked up her things and headed for the door.

'Vasudha?'

'Yes, sir?'

'Could you make sure the Do Not Disturb is working? I haven't slept for eighteen hours and need a break.'

'Certainly sir. Happy dreams.'

She stepped out and found herself shaking slightly as she set his room to DND status.

TWO

It was around one in the afternoon before Vasudha could take a break in the employees' room. Maddy beckoned to her.

'Been waiting for those parathas.'

'Haai, how much you can eat!' said Trilok Sadhu, an elderly man who liked to say that he had spent his life in the service of the hotel.

'I'm not eating any of yours,' said Maddy.

'One should not talk like that about food, Sadhu sir,' said Vasudha quietly. 'There is no savour to food that cannot be shared.'

'Well said,' said Sadhu. 'And I hope to see you at the annual staff celebration. It's also a potluck, you see.'

'I'm sorry, Sadhu sir, I don't think I'll be coming.'

'Arrey, why not?' Maddy asked.

'How can a woman come to a party when her husband is not around?' Vasudha said, and Maddy rolled her eyes.

'And where is your husband?' Sadhu asked.

'Posted abroad,' she said briefly.

'You know he may well be partying with some other woman,' said Sadhu, winking at her. 'You should not waste your youth.'

Vasudha got up abruptly.

'Oho baba, it is only a joke,' said Sadhu uncomfortably as he looked at her. Had he really said something that would cost him his job? One never knew these days.

'My marriage is not a joke,' said Vasudha.

'You na, Sadhu!' said Maddy irritably. 'You think you can say anything or what? Even if there was one per cent chance she might come, now that's dead and gone.'

And then the fire alarm began to sound, a harsh insistent screaming.

Sadhu was the first to leap to his feet and run out.

'Look, look at him—he has spent his life in the service of this hotel but he's the first to run!' said Maddy. 'Chalo baba, we should also move.'

Vasudha turned to leave when she saw a huge bouquet with a tag attached: For Mr Aarav Ruparel.

'Maddy?'

'Haan?'

'That man, that Aarav Ruparel?'

'What about him?'

'His room is DND. It's been sound-proofed for guests. He might not hear the alarm.'

'Cool, it's only a fire drill,' Maddy began when suddenly a shrill voice shouted, *'Arrey, suchmuch aag lagi hai!'*

Maddy grabbed Vasudha's arm.

'Let's go.'

'But he…'

'Tell a security guard, isn't it their job?'

Outside it was chaos as streams of hotel staff and guests came pouring out onto the manicured lawn. They all turned to stare at the smoke issuing from the hotel.

'It looks like that Taj Mahal, na?' someone said and immediately a few media-minded souls began to take pictures and whatsapp them to their friends. The staff tried to make order but there were many reluctant diners who were worried about their food. 'I will not pay for the wine,' said a man. 'Please send your manager.' One corpulent soul had brought his plate with him and now nibbled on Chicken a la Kiev as he sat on the grass. Others scuttled off, happy not to be paying their bills. A French woman was worried sick about her jewellery. 'It's on the bed. I just ran when the alarm sounded. I hope the firemen of India are honest.'

Vasudha located a security guard.

'We have a guest in the Presidential suite,' she began.

'Arre chhodo madam,' he said. 'I'm not risking my life for a twenty-thousand-rupee job.'

Vasudha began to run towards the hotel.

'Where are you going?' Maddy shouted at her.

'I'm going for him,' Vasudha shouted back.

'Don't take the lift,' Maddy instructed. 'You're not supposed to take the lift in case of a fire.'

Vasudha thanked her stars that the Presidential Suite was only on the third floor. The smoke seemed thickest here and she stuffed the end of her sari against her nose. Using her All-Access Card, she opened the door.

'Sir!' she shouted as she entered the suite. 'Mr Ruparel? Wake up sir, wake up. The hotel is on fire!'

She plunged towards the bedroom.

'Nine minutes,' came a composed voice behind her.

She whirled around. Aarav was sitting on the sofa, dressed in jeans and a t-shirt. His face was covered in a gas mask. In one hand, he carried a stopwatch which he turned off now with a definitive click before setting it down. He picked up his iPhone and dialled a number.

'Apoorva, turn off that smoke machine.'

Then he smiled at her.

'Use the intercom or whatever you want. Calm the guests, get them back into their rooms or into the bar or the swimming pool or wherever they were. Announce that they can have their meal free or the day free or whatever it is.'

He walked to the window and looked out.

'Also tell the gentlemen of the press that there is no scandal, no terrorist attack, nothing but a fire drill played out in a suitably dramatic manner.'

Vasudha turned to go.

'And get me the Head of Housekeeping, the Head of Security, the General Manager and whatever senior-level staff can be spared from the duty of soothing ruffled feathers into the boardroom.'

'Yes, sir.'

'And I want you to be there.'

'Me, sir?'

'You. Thank you, that will be all.'

At that moment, the door opened and Apoorva, his close friend, walked in.

'Apoorva, I would like you to meet the only person in this hotel who has internalised the motto of the Indian hospitality industry: atithi devo bhava.'

'It's too late in the afternoon for Sanskrit,' said Apoorva.

'Our guest is as our god,' said Vasudha.

'You know Sanskrit?'

'I'm no Monier-Williams sir, but…'

'Now who is that?' asked Apoorva.

'He's the gent who wrote a fine Sanskrit-English dictionary,' said Aarav.

'His first name was also Monier,' said Vasudha. 'Can you imagine? Monier Monier-Williams?'

Aarav laughed.

'Really?'

Apoorva cleared his throat ostentatiously.

'Is he coming to this meeting too?'

Aarav began to laugh and saw Vasudha control a smile.

'That would be quite something. He's been dead a while.'

Vasudha slipped out of the room and Aarav smiled at Apoorva.

'The media want you to talk to them,' said Apoorva.

'The media wants the moon. Go and show them a reflection on a plate,' said Aarav. 'Now I've got to try and look like a businessman.'

~

When Aarav and Apoorva entered the room, a hush fell.

'Good afternoon, gentlemen, ladies,' said Aarav. 'Or rather, a bad afternoon for the hotel. You ran like headless chickens when there was a guest in your hotel.'

'Sir...' one of the black suits began.

'No. Don't say anything. Just listen. If a hotel is worth anything at all, it isn't because of the number of Michelin stars its restaurants have or how many heads of state have lived there. Because that is history. And while history is of deep interest to me, it is the present and the future on which I stake my money. I have just spent a good deal of money on acquiring this hotel. And so one of the first things I do when I arrive is: I run a little test. And what do I find? Almost every one of you is found wanting. You run *away* from the guests rather than to them.'

He paused and let his words sink in.

'With one exception.' He pointed to Vasudha. 'That lady, Vasudha, over there. The flower lady. She thinks fit to walk up three flights of stairs to get to my room and get me out of it. That is what I call service. That is what any guest would call service, not the number of chocolates you tuck under their coverlets or how many shampoo bottles you put in their bathrooms for them to steal...though in India, I am told that counts for quite a lot too.'

Vasudha chuckled and everyone turned to look at her. Then they realised that Aarav had made a joke and they laughed too, a little too loud, a little too long. He seemed to recognise it too, Vasudha noticed, for his hand went up to quell the laughter.

'You may all take it that you are on notice,' he said.

There was a gasp.

'Yes. I'm giving you all six months' time to get your act together, to learn to act as if the hotel means something to you, to find ways in which to make the clients happier than they have been, to redefine service and to reinvent standards.'

'Sir?' said Leena.

'Yes?'

'How about if we were to put real plants, living plants in all the rooms instead of flowers? That would give the guests a sense of coming into a room that is already lived in.'

'That is a fine idea, Leena-ji. Is it your own?'

'Yes, sir,' said Leena and studiously avoided looking at Vasudha.

'It is such a good idea that I am going to ask all the one hundred and eight hotels in my chain to implement it,' said Aarav. Leena looked delighted.

'But I am also going to ask you to hand in your resignation,' he said. 'I hate people who steal ideas from their subordinates and pass them off as their own. That is one sure way to spread disaffection.'

There is a dead silence.

'You may leave now, Leena-ji,' said Aarav. 'The rest of the meeting is for the senior management of the hotel.'

Leena grabbed her bag and ran for the door blindly. The rest of the meeting was formulaic, with the senior management trying to gauge the temperature and pressure at which their new boss worked and discovering that he seemed to be a living example of some kind of physical law: his decision-making process was cold as outer space, his demands were as high-pressure as the centre of the earth. When it was over, they were all sweating despite the air-conditioning. Many were planning to look for jobs in other hotels.

'And now, ladies and gentlemen, I suggest you all go away and think about this meeting,' said Aarav.

'Apoorva, my right hand man, will take another meeting tomorrow which I call The Ideas Event. If you don't have a new idea, don't show up for the event. But don't show up for work either. Kemo?'

There were reluctant nods all round.

'Vasudha, I'd like you to stay after all the rest leave.'

It was not a hint; it was a directive. With a general rustling, the senior management prepared to leave.

'You have three things I want of those on the team who reports directly to me. One is that you have new ideas. Second, you have total commitment. Third, you don't seem terrified of me. Your new assignment begins today. You have a passport?'

'Sir...' Vasudha began. She could see Apoorva reaching for his iPad to make notes.

'Doesn't matter if you don't have one but here's something I want you to internalise. We must all prepare for success. If you don't have a passport, that's a way of telling the universe that you don't want to travel, you don't want to see the world, you don't want to spread your wings. So everyone should have a passport.'

'Sir, I need to...'

'Don't worry about what you need. My team comes fully equipped. Everything you need and want will be yours. You will lack for nothing.'

'Sir...'

'I leave this evening. I don't think you can possibly make that flight. But I will expect...'

Now Vasudha was close to desperate.

'I'm sorry, Sir, but I will have to refuse your kind offer,' she broke in. In the corner of her eye she could see surprise break over Apoorva's face. It was obvious that Mr Ruparel was not in the habit of being refused, not even when he was seeking to rewrite someone's life.

'I have a son. He goes to school here. I have a life that allows me to come home to him and be his mother. I don't *want* to change any of that,' she said. 'I don't *need* to change any of that.'

Aarav looked at her for a moment. A decade of poker games with high stakes—as he had once described business deals to Apoorva—had made him the master of his face but for a moment hurt and surprise peeked through. 'Hurt?' He asked himself now, 'why am I hurt? I offer a phoolwali a job and she turns it down. She has the Indian disease: a lack of ambition, a chalta hai attitude. I thought she was different. She is, but not in the way I need her to be.' Then something else said inside him, 'You know that's not true. There is something rare here, rare and clean. This is like a mountain spring after you have been drinking brackish water by the sea. You know this and you should also know that it is only your hurt speaking.'

But before he could quell his hurt, it was already forcing him to say: 'I rarely make the same offer twice.'

Vasudha smiled and said, 'I am honoured by your offer, sir. And I will always remember it but I don't think I will be changing my mind.'

'But on the other hand,' he added smoothly, 'because of your rare combination of skills and talents, I'm willing to make an exception. My offer will remain open for you.'

Apoorva now looked as if the world had shifted on its axis and the magnetic meridians were being rewritten. Vasudha smiled again and left the room.

Inside, Apoorva said, 'Mr I-Only-Offer-Once, I hope you're still thinking with your head.'

'And what do you think I might be thinking with?' Aarav asked wryly, bracing himself.

'Some parts south of your belt,' said Apoorva.

Aarav smiled.

THREE

Outside the board room, Vasudha took a deep breath in order to still her madly racing pulse. Why did the man have such an effect on her? 'You are a married woman,' she said. 'You are an Indian married woman. You have a tradition to uphold…'

Inside her, a rebellious voice said, 'Is there a tradition for Indian married men, too? Do they get to play by the same rules? Do they get offered a bunch of dependable reliable men as role models who loved their wives to devotion and never strayed? Were there ever such men?'

And then her thoughts were disrupted as the lift door opened and Maddy came running out.

'Arrey, where all I have looked for you! Is your phone off or something?'

'No, I put it on silent because we had a board meeting with the bosses.'

'Arrey, Saanjh…'

Panic burst inside Vasudha but she had learned that as a single parent, panic was not an option. She squashed it and said, 'What about Saanjh? What has happened to him?'

'He's not in school. The police have picked him up and taken him to the Head Office of the Crime Branch.'

'What!'

'The principal was saying, some Inspector called Vinod Patil came for him and took him away.'

'Vinod Patil?'

'How they can do things like that, I don't know…'

But Vasudha was already running down the corridor.

Outside, the security guard was looking dismal. He had been asked, no doubt, to explain his behaviour. But he got Vasudha a cab. All the way to the Crime Branch, Vasudha felt the city turn into a cesspool, a chamber of horrors, a snake pit. The child begging at the taxi window became the symbol of all children who were denied their rights. The woman crossing the road with a huge load on her head became all women who had to deal with more than their fair share of the work while being denied their share of the world's goods. The boy with a catapult became a sign of how casual masculine cruelty could be. This was no city to bring up a child. This was no way to bring up a child. How could the school have…? How could the police have…? What had Hari done now that…? The questions came and went in wave after wave of worry.

~

'Madam? Pahunch gaye.'

She reached blindly into her purse and pulled out her emergency five-hundred-rupee note.

'Madam, change dijiye.'

For a moment, she wanted to shout, 'Keep it!' but she could not afford to. There were expenses this month and Saanjh would expect a birthday treat tonight. She fished the money out and then ran half-blind into the building. She did not notice its stern Victorian beauty. She did not even notice the masses of bougainvillaea that were blooming over the walls. She ran straight up to the reception and demanded, 'Where is my son?'

The policeman looked up at her, bored. 'Everyone here is someone's son. How would I know which one is yours?'

Vasudha wanted to shriek at him but she stopped herself.

'Saanjh…' and even as she said it she knew that it would mean nothing to him. One very small boy in this very large building. How could they even think…? 'I mean, Inspector Vinod Patil. I want to meet Inspector Vinod Patil.'

There was a slight shift in his demeanour as if the name itself held some kind of magic.

'Say like that. Shouting where is my son. First floor, third cabin.'

Vasudha ran to the staircase.

'Madam, there is a lift.'

Vasudha knew that it probably made more sense to wait for the lift but there was something urgent inside her that was impelling her forward, making her limbs impatient, turning her into an impractical person. She could not wait for a lift even if it meant that she would get there faster. And as she got to the first floor, she noticed that the lift was even now beginning its slow and government-paced descent to the ground floor.

Inspector Patil's cabin door was open and there was Saanjh. He was not weeping, he was not handcuffed, he was not bloodied…and only now, as she noted that he was not any of these things, did she allow herself to confront what her fears had been.

'Hey Maa,' Saanjh looked up. 'This is a real good computer, Maa. Papa should have got me this model.' There was a small birthday cake next to the computer, and a bottle of Mirinda, half full.

'Come in Mrs Hari Prasad,' said Inspector Patil, gesturing to an inner room. 'We can leave young Saanjh here to play his video games while you and I talk.'

'Take your time, Maa,' said Saanjh expansively as he settled back at the computer.

'What is the meaning of this? Aren't you ashamed picking up a child like this, a mere child! Has the police now decided to…' Vasudha began as soon as they had entered the inner room.

Inspector Patil cut in. 'The police has not decided to do anything other than to do its duty. And if doing that duty requires us to pick up a schoolboy and bring him here, we will do that. But I do not think that young Saanjh is complaining, do you? He seems rather happy to be here.'

Vasudha found herself speechless in the face of such urbanity and such a complete lack of guilt.

'This is not the way,' she muttered.

'What is the way then? Do you have some good ideas about the best way to deal with terrorists, Mrs Hari Prasad?'

He keeps using Hari's name, Vasudha thought. Oh Hari, what have you gone and done?

Something of her concern must have shown on her face, for she could sense a difference in the police officer in front of her.

His tone now became that of the interrogating officer.

'Is your name Vasudha Hari Prasad?'

'It is.'

'Is your husband Hari Raghunath Prasad?'

'It is.'

'Is this the said man, Hari Raghunath Prasad?'

She looked down at the grainy black-and-white photograph which he waved under her nose.

'It is.'

'When did you last have contact with the said Hari Raghunath Prasad?'

She tried to think back. When had she last seen the man?

'Five years ago?'

'By contact, I do not only mean physical contact. I also mean when did he last get in touch with you?'

She tried to remember the time that Hari had slammed out of the door, announcing that he had a job and that he couldn't be bothered with all the small stuff that kept him in the city. He had said that he was going to drive some posh people around in Orissa and he would make enough money to relax for the rest of the year. Vasudha had wanted to tell him that no job, no honest job, ever paid that kind of money. But a few years into her marriage she had learned to leave well alone, not to argue with him, not to ever correct him or check him in anything he wanted to do. Like Kate in Shakespeare's play, she had learned to let him play Petruchio. If it were night and he said it was day, then it was day. If he said the sky was green and the grass was blue, that was correct too. If she tried to contradict him or correct him or check him, Hari immediately started to shout. This made her heart sink because she knew that the shouting only presaged the beating. And when her heart sank, she lost the desire to argue. This only enraged Hari more, for he thought of it as her sulking.

'Don't throw your airs and graces at me,' he would say. 'Talk to me, you slut.'

But if she opened her mouth, that too was wrong.

'Oh now you think you can teach me, do you?' And the blows would follow.

Once her mother-in-law had tried to intervene and Hari had lashed out at the old lady too. Afterwards, as Vasudha applied liniment to the old lady's aching bones, she had said, 'His father was exactly like that.' The women's eyes had met in a moment of understanding. They had both lived with the threat of blows and beatings. The threat of those blows locked her mouth but they also made them inevitable. And so when Hari had stormed out of the house that day, Vasudha had known a rare moment of relief. She had found herself praying that the posh people would take their time, would want to wander through Orissa.

Then the weeks had passed, and the months, and she had found a job in a florist's shop. The old florist had recommended her name to the hotel and when she had found regular work, she had also moved Hari's mother into an old age home at the old lady's insistence.

'I cannot live where my son does not live,' she had said. Vasudha had opened her mouth to insist but the old lady had given her a quick smile. 'That is what I will tell the world. My child, this family has done enough damage to you. I will not be an additional burden. But you must promise me one thing.'

'Tell me,' said Vasudha.

'You must bring him to see me,' she said pointing at the baby in Vasudha's arms. 'He is the future, my future. And I will pray that he will be a better future for both of us than the men who have defined our lives till now.'

'Madam, I am asking you to think about your answer,' came Inspector Patil's voice, with a trace of irritation now.

'I haven't seen my husband for nearly five years. Nor have I spoken to him. Nor has he contacted me in any way.'

'No?'

'You are one hundred per cent sure?'

'I am.'

'Do you know what your husband has been up to?'

She wanted to say: 'How could I know when he has not been in touch?' but she thought better of it and kept her answer simple. 'No.'

'Then let me tell you. He has been involved in the kidnapping of an American couple.'

'What?'

'Yes. They have been held for ransom in Bastar.'

'Hari?'

'Now you will say, 'My Hari?' as if he is a saint. Every woman says the same thing. The mothers say it about their sons. The daughters say it about their fathers. The wives say it about their husbands.'

Vasudha felt the same way but for different reasons. The man she had married was capable of violence, it was true. But could he plan and execute something like a kidnapping? There was so much you needed. A gun, perhaps. A place to hide the hostages, a safe place. Someone to feed them. Someone to organise the ransom demands. Someone to pick up the money. Hari? He had not been able to make himself a cup of tea on those days when she had not stepped into the kitchen because her father had told her that she would pollute it. Hari might be a pawn in someone else's game, lured in by the promises of big money, but as for political beliefs, he had none. He didn't even read the newspaper in the morning, preferring, as she remembered it, the more sensational news channels and their relentless coverage of sex murders and bizarre animals born in the hinterland.

'You see?'

Vasudha didn't.

'This is why we have brought your son here.'

Vasudha still didn't see.

'*Khud doond rahi hai shama jisse, kya baat hai us parwaane ki,*' said Patil. 'You came to us. We did not have to come to you.'

'This is the first I have heard of Hari being involved in something like this.'

Patil pretended to look as if he understood.

'Ah, and that is because he has not been in touch with you.'

'Yes.'

'Then what is this?' Inspector Patil produced a sheet of paper and waved it under her nose. Vasudha looked down at it and recognised the note she had written for her son. She wanted to laugh hysterically.

'This is a fake,' she said. 'I wrote it. I wrote it so that my son would not think that his father had forgotten about him again on his birthday.'

'And he believed it?'

'He did.'

Patil looked out through the transparent glass panel. Saanjh was still engrossed in his game.

'That's a very intelligent child you have there. He seems to have a natural bond with the computer.'

Vasudha's heart swelled with pride.

'Yes, he is.'

'And he was fooled by this forgery?'

'You are a lucky man, Inspector, if you do not know that sometimes we will allow our hearts to be fooled to spare us pain.'

'This letter is enough for me to...'

Vasudha picked up a pen and wrote a few words in the same handwriting. Then she pulled out a bill from her handbag. It was the bill for the computer.

'This is what I bought for him. His father's birthday gift.'

A moment of doubt crossed Patil's face. Vasudha saw it and decided to risk it all.

'I think you have made a grave mistake in bringing a child into a police station. I think you have made an even more stupid mistake in trying to interrogate me. I will not tolerate it,' she said.

Patil looked at her and for a moment he saw a line of warrior queens, Razia Sultana to Rani Lakshmibai.

'I would not leave the city if I were you,' he said.

'But you are not me, Inspector, and I warn you, my son is going to boarding school in...' she thought desperately, quickly, 'Singapore and I am taking up my new assignment in Dubai.'

Patil began to frown.

'You had better...'

'No, Inspector, if you want you can make it difficult for me to leave the country. I understand that. You have only to start an investigation. But I shall step out of here and I shall go to the *Times of India* and I shall tell the reporters there how you took an innocent boy out of school and then interrogated his mother with no woman police-person in the room. I shall speak to the People's Union for Civil Liberties and the Women's Cell. I shall knock on every door and I shall do whatever I can to make sure I secure my son's future against further incursions into his privacy and mine. Know this, Inspector—Hari is my husband, and as my husband he has every right to my respect, but no right to my love. He has abandoned me. That I could forgive. But he has abandoned his son as well. That I cannot forgive. You could have called me here. Instead, you used my son. That is just not on. Now if you do not intend to arrest us, I'm taking my son and I am leaving.'

'Mrs Prasad?'

'Yes?'

'It is never a good idea to threaten a policeman,' said Inspector Patil but his voice was mild.

'Inspector Patil, you should learn that it is always a good idea to threaten a woman. We are trained to quail. But it is never wise to threaten a mother. We are trained to protect and defend.'

Vasudha rose. She looked him straight in the eye.

'I will be leaving for Dubai soon and my son will be leaving for Singapore. I would advise you not to stand in my way.'

She stepped out.

'Saanjh!' she called.

The boy looked up, a protest on his lips. He had a level to complete. He had a game to win. But when his mother used a certain tone of voice, he knew better than to argue. He rose immediately and went to her side.

'Say goodbye to the kind Inspector,' said Vasudha keeping her tone free of any irony.

'See you later, kid,' said Inspector Patil.

FOUR

Outside the police station she wanted to take a cab home but she did not dare. It would be a signal to Saanjh that something was wrong. Instead, she decided to take him to see his grandmother.

'It is time for our annual visit and we can make it there and back in time for a pizza,' she said.

'Pizza! Homemade?'

She sighed. Try as she might her pizzas did not seem to stack up against the commercial stuff.

'It's your birthday. We'll order in.'

'Yay!' he said and then amended it immediately. 'I mean I love your pizzas too, Maa…'

'No need to lie. Your heart belongs to Pizza Parlour,' she said and smiled at him.

When they got off the bus at the old age home, the matron smiled. 'She's having a good day,' she said and led them to the old lady's bed where she seemed to be dozing in the late evening sun. It was enough to see her eyes light up with joy at the sight of her grandchild. Vasudha left them to have a few minutes alone and went for a walk. When she returned, her mother-in-law was no longer recumbent. She was sitting bolt upright in bed and her eyes were like lasers.

'The cat has had another litter of kittens, Saanjh. Go play with them.'

Saanjh threw her an apologetic look as he departed.

'Police? The police come to his school and take him with them?'

Vasudha looked at the old woman and wondered where this fire had been banked when she had been a mute witness to the beatings, the marital rape, the constant affray. But she said only, 'I've sorted that out.'

The old woman suddenly deflated.

'Hari?'

Vasudha nodded.

'Bad seed. My father called him bad seed. I had laughed then, but I know now.'

Vasudha sat down beside her and said, 'Then Saanjh is also damned.'

'No,' said the old lady. 'I have faith in you. I have faith in the kind of family you can provide for him. I have faith in the future.'

'And I must safeguard that faith.'

The old lady looked sharply at her.

'Hari is now wanted by the police. To get him, they

picked up Saanjh. They may do it again. They may not do it so kindly. I want him out of the country.'

The old lady nodded slowly. 'But where?' she asked.

'I've been offered a job in Dubai. I'll see if that will cover the cost of his education in Singapore.'

'What kind of job?' the old lady asked and then shrugged. 'No, I don't want to know. I only want him safe.'

'It may be difficult for him to meet you every year.'

The old woman's shoulders sagged.

'You will do what is right. That is what I know about you. You will do it at whatever the cost.'

Vasudha wanted to weep and lay her head on the old woman's shoulder. But there was too much hurt, too much distrust and betrayal between them. She had hoped when she married Hari to find a mother in his mother. She had found a witness; a sympathetic one, yes, but only a witness.

'When do you leave?'

'As soon as I can.'

'When does he leave?'

'Before me.'

The old lady nodded. Then she laid her head on Vasudha's bosom. She saw the mangalsutra gleaming there.

'Why do you wear that? It has brought you nothing but grief.'

'It brought me Saanjh,' said Vasudha.

'Yes. But why are you still waiting for that demon? It's been five years, how many more years of your life will you waste, Vasu? I carried him in my womb, but he was his father's spawn. The pujari's son. That pujari broke my bones many times—once because he caught me eating an onion with my roti. His son watched and learned well. Have you forgotten what he did to you?'

'No, I haven't,' Vasudha said. 'And I remember that you always had a neighbour to visit when it started.'

'I was scared, Vasu. He is his father's son. Do you think he would have spared me only because I am his mother? He locked me out of the house one night because I returned late from work. I cleaned the airport floors to feed him and put him through school and college, and he locked me out because he thought...' the old lady broke down.

'I'm sorry, Maa ji. I don't blame you. But I'm still his wife. Neither of us can change that. Just promise me you will take care of yourself. And call me anytime you need something. Dubai is not very far.'

The old lady nodded and smiled through her tears. 'Don't worry about me. You've done so much for me already.' She held Vasudha's hand and kissed it. 'Bring Saanjh to me. I want to hold him for a moment. It may be all I have to go on for a long time.'

Saanjh was playing outside with a kitten.

'Look, Maa, she likes me,' he said, holding the little ball of grey fur close to his chest. 'Can we take her with us? I'll keep her in my school bag so that she's never alone.'

'No,' said Vasudha. 'You can't have the kitten. Give her a last kiss and go back to your grandmother. Stay with her for a while. I'll pick you up later.'

'Where are you going?'

'I have a meeting.'

~

On the way back to the hotel, Vasudha tried to formulate a nice speech of acceptance. But when she arrived at Aarav Ruparel's office, her heart was fluttering madly again. She pushed open the door. Apoorva was there and gestured her in.

'He will see me?'

'He's been expecting you.'

She went into Aarav's room but as she went in, she pulled the mangalsutra out of hiding and placed it on top of her sari's pallu. Vasudha knew she was doing this as much for herself as for him.

'Ah,' said Aarav. 'When can you start?'

'I need to make some things clear,' Vasudha said in a voice unusually firm, to hide the trembling. 'I'm a married woman. My husband has been missing for several years. I have a son. His education cannot continue in this city. I want him to study in Singapore.'

Aarav had been looking at her, unblinking. It was the look of Aarav Ruparel at a business meeting. Now he raised a hand.

'His name?'

'Saanjh Hari Prasad.'

He picked up his iPhone and dialled.

'Anand? Favour time.'

There was a chuckle on the other end.

'No, it's not business. I just need an admission into that school you own in Singapore, for a Saanjh Hari Prasad. His transcripts will be with you ASAP.'

He paused.

'Great. I owe you.'

Then he turned to her.

'Now do you want us to find your husband?' His voice was flat, without emotion.

'No,' Vasudha said. She wanted to add something and Aarav obviously expected it because he did not say a word and kept looking at her. But she could not say anything.

'What is it? Are you afraid he has another wife and another family?'

Vasudha wanted to laugh. But she knew she had to tell this man the truth. For some reason it was very important that he should know everything.

'Hari seems to be under suspicion. I thought he was a driver. But the police think he has helped kidnap some American tourists. Something to do with the Maoists.'

There was a pause. When she looked at him, his eyes pierced hers.

'Is that why you want to get out of the country?' he asked.

'Today my son was picked up by the police. An eight-year-old. An innocent eight-year-old. Because I faked a letter from his father to back up a birthday present I bought in his name. My son and I have nothing to do with Hari or what he has been doing. I promise you that. But I want him to grow up safe.'

He looked at her, long and hard. Suddenly, she could see the steel in him, the unrelenting businessman who was used to taking in data and people and personalities and qualities and opportunities and turning all of that into money. But she faced his stare with steady eyes. She did not flinch because she had told him the truth.

'Okay,' he said. 'Even if it is true that he has kidnapped those tourists, I can't see that it has anything to do with you. Go on to Personnel and get your paperwork done. Sign the form for the Tatkaal passport that Apoorva has prepared for you. Does Saanjh have a passport?

'No.'

'Tell Apoorva to get him one too. You and your son will have an appointment tomorrow morning with the passport office. Tell Apoorva to add Saanjh's name to the Ministry when he sends the email. Get yourself some new clothes. Take Naila's number down. She will be your contact. Tell Apoorva to get Naila on your case. I'll be leaving in six hours. Get a new phone. That one won't do. I want you on whatsapp with me. There are two pre-approved credit cards in that case. Take them and go and make your pin changes. Report back to me when all of the above are done.'

Vasudha felt that it was her first test as she got through the next two hours, but none of this mattered. She signed the forms blindly, changed the PIN on the cards, discovered that she had been paid a month's salary in advance and for a moment almost gasped aloud at the figure. It was more money than she had ever earned in her life. But none of this actually touched her. She was only worried about how Saanjh would react to the changes she was going to inflict on his life.

And when she switched on her new phone, her first whatsapp message appeared from Aarav. 'Tell Saanjh you will get so many air miles that you will be able to visit him free in Singapore for every school holiday or he can come and see you in Dubai. Or wherever you're posted.'

It was at that moment that Vasudha knew she was dangerously close to falling in love with Aarav Ruparel.

FIVE

It was not even two days later that Vasudha found herself on an Air India flight to Dubai. She wanted to sleep, because she knew that it was late in the night, but she couldn't. Things had moved at the speed of light.

The conversation with Saanjh had come close to destroying her resolve. The boy had wept as if his heart would break. But when she found herself weakening, she thought back to the moment when she had seen her son in Inspector Patil's cabin and she had steeled herself and taken his crying form into her arms and said, 'My darling, one day you'll know the pain of sending your child far away from you, but you will also understand why I have to do this. Help me do what is right, Saanjh.'

And then there was a knock on the door. Vasudha opened it and found Apoorva there. He was carrying a parcel.

'What is it?' she asked.

'It's a delivery. The boy's dad sent it.'

'My father?' Saanjh looked up. He came to the door, his face tear-stained.

Apoorva came in and put the box down.

'Go on. Open it,' he said. Saanjh turned to his mother with a mute appeal. Vasudha nodded.

Inside was a laptop. And within minutes, Saanjh was entranced and the journey to Singapore had taken on another dimension altogether.

Apoorva smiled and left. That was only the beginning. Her passport was sent to her within the day. Saanjh's clothes for his Singapore school had been arranged. Saanjh loved the school jacket. He tried it out in front of the mirror, but he was crying. Vasudha watched from a distance, a knife in her heart. And then she saw him wipe his eyes and stand quite still, looking hard at his reflection. He seemed to be processing information.

In the middle of the night, he came to Vasudha and said, 'Maa.'

She was awake immediately.

'Saanjh beta? What?'

'You will be safe, Maa. Those men won't be there. And I will study hard and do well and make you a home.'

For years, she had had to manage by herself. And now there seemed to be two men who in their different ways were offering her their unstinting support. That night, she buried her nose in Saanjh's hair and tried to fill her lungs with the scent of the child she was sending away.

The next morning, there was another surprise.

Maddy had arrived at her home, bubbling with excitement.

'You know what? They're sending me to Singapore! With Saanjh. I'm going as escort! Thank God, I made my passport some time back only. My first time, you know. So I'm going with one fully empty sooty...'

'Sooty?' asked Vasudha, puzzled.

'Arre, suitcase. I'm taking one list. Everyone wants this and that from Mustafa or Orchard Road. I'll do full shopping. You want something...uff ho, where is my head? You're going to Fly Buy Dubai. What will *you* want? Your kismet is full chamko right now, girl—and some shine is falling on me!'

It seemed that Aarav had thought of everything.

Now in the airplane with its aseptic smells, it was only an elusive memory. She was in free fall now, with almost nothing to hold on to. She had no flowers to cushion her. She had no schedule to envelop her. She had no son to cook for. She only had a passport and a phone number for someone called Naila. If she were not at the airport, Vasudha did not know what she would do. She had never flown before, never mind flown internationally. And she wasn't even sure how the phones worked abroad. She didn't know what her job designation was. She didn't know...

Completely exhausted, she fell asleep.

~

The airhostess woke her up, not too gently, and asked her to set her chair upright and raise her window shades, preparatory for landing. The tensions of the night before returned in a rush. But in the next few minutes, she realised that there was nothing she had to do except to follow the crowd of Indians getting off the aircraft. She followed a group of young Malayali girls who were chattering to each other almost as if coming to Dubai was like taking a bus in Allapuzha. She envied their insouciance and effortless cosmopolitanism. She hoped Saanjh and Maddy were managing too.

The unfamiliar sounds of an airport caught her again by surprise. It made her feel the airplane was a safe space in which she had been cocooned for a while. And as she hurried along, her steps taking on the urgency of the other people walking, she found herself wondering, 'What am I doing here? What was I thinking? How will this work? What if this doesn't work? What if I can't do the work I'm supposed to? What if I can't explain the flowers I want to the suppliers?'

But then she was at the carousel and her old battered suitcase, the same one she had carried from her father's house to Hari's home, was coming around. Oddly, it reassured her. It had come through intact. And she would too.

Outside, the day was warm and someone came up and tapped her on the shoulder.

'Vasudha?'

She turned around and was greeted by a pair of sparkling eyes.

'Naila Sarwar?'

'At your service,' said Naila. 'And by that I mean, anything you need or want, you just let me know and I'll make it happen.'

'At this point in time, I need a SIM card,' said Vasudha. 'An international SIM card.'

'Khul ja SIM-SIM,' said Naila. 'Your wish is my command.' And her phone started to ring. It was a Hindi film song.

'My jaanu is remembering me,' she said, switching to English and began to dig in her capacious handbag. 'Hello chweechie,' she said. 'Mwah-Mwah-Mwah.'

Vasudha stepped away, out of earshot. The rest of the conversation seemed to consist of words that had been mauled out of shape to make them sound sweeter to the ear or sounds that were supposed to represent kisses of various kinds. But eventually it did get over and Naila came back, her eyes triumphant and defiant at the same time.

'Your husband?' Vasudha asked politely.

'Husband? He toh is sitting in Lahore, eating kababs on my money and doing aish. No, this is my chaahanewaala,' Naila said. 'His name is George. He's from Goa. So we're doing our bit for Indo-Pak friendship.'

Vasudha did not know what to say to this.

'He's also married. And he loves his begum, as I love my Lahore-wala, in case you're thinking I don't. And maybe his begum is also eating kababs on his money and watching TV all day! No, but I don't think she's like that. She seems like Mother India. He showed me her photoo. She looked very strick.'

Vasudha wondered whether Naila needed to confess all these things or whether she was simply the kind of person who told you about her life on the first encounter. Looking at the pretty and disingenuous face, she decided it was probably a little of both.

'I work in the housekeeping department of the Hotel Noor-e Dubai,' Naila continued. 'And I am your lie-zone.'

'Sorry?' Vasudha was genuinely puzzled by this.

'Lie-zone yaar, these English words are too bore. Am I saying it all wrong then?'

'Liaison?' suggested Vasudha.

'Ajeeb thing this Angrezi. Spelling is going Tokyo pronounciation is looking London. But what to do na— whether in Lahore or in Dilli or in Dubai we have to bark in this zaleel language. Nahi toh no good pay, no rich lovers. I'm third-class fail, but at least I can speak ten-twelve words. Only pronounciation is a fat-bum-size problem.'

'Pronunciation,' Vasudha corrected her gently.

'Haan, you correct my English-Vinglish and I will show you how to do Dubai. Best shopping? Ask Naila. Best shawarma? Ask Naila. Best of the rest, ask Naila.'

And she gave Vasudha a nudge and a wink that left nothing to the imagination.

'Naila,' said Vasudha gently. 'I think we can be friends, but only if we get one thing straight.'

'Haan. Bolo. I am all for straight.'

'I don't drink. I don't smoke. I don't eat non-vegetarian.'

'Beda garak! Toh what fun you are having in life?'

'I manage, thank you. I have my son and my work.'

'And Aarav.'

'Sorry?'

'Arrey full Dubai knows the story of how he is fidaa over you.'

'Full Dubai is wrong then. Mr Ruparel does not hire people because he is fidaa over them.'

'Don't get me wrong, jaanu. I don't care,' said Naila. 'But see it this way. Here you are, without hi-fi-degree. I think you're twelfth standard pass, maximum BA-Shee-A, right? Not even MBA type, I think. Not even from some dantmanjan college, na? And you are, a member of Mr Aarav Ruparel's team! If that is not called being fidaa then I don't know what is.'

She caught sight of Vasudha's face, which was a study in conflicting emotions.

'Uff! I toh am too mooh-phat. My mother used to say to me, "One day, Naila, you will open your mouth and swallow full Lahore." And she's right. Don't listen to me, haan? And this is where you can get your SIM card.'

As Vasudha dealt with the matter of the SIM card, she thought about what Naila had said. She had never thought of her hiring as anything but a matter of...of what? She knew she was not equipped to handle much more than flowers and yet, here she was in Dubai. She had taken the job only to get away from it all—from Patil and Anil and Samson and yes, from Hari too. She tried to enumerate to herself again the reasons that Aarav had given her for hiring her. He had been serious. He had seen something in her, perhaps something she had not seen in herself. Yes, she told herself firmly. She had earned her place here and she would work hard, with the Devi by her side and her mother's blessings at her back and her son's future front and centre of her mind.

So why did she feel this tiny warm trickle of delight at the thought that Aarav had chosen her because he was, in Naila's words, fidaa over her?

SIX

In truth Aarav was asking himself the same questions. He had invented a series of plausible reasons to do what he wanted to do, which was to be in the same country, in the same city, in the same room with Vasudha. No, he wanted more than that, he had to admit. He wanted *her*.

And oddly, he wanted her in a strange way that went beyond the carnal. He wanted to be inside her, yes, but not just inside her body. He wanted to prowl the byways of her mind. He wanted to know what went on in her heart. He wanted to understand her spirit, what made her apologise to flowers and want to turn hotel rooms into homes. He wanted to drag her from behind her mask; he wanted to break the reins with which she held her senses in check. He wanted her to be available to him at all times and wondered whether that would rid him of the sensual thrall he felt he was in when he saw her.

It did not help that he sensed, without even having to

ask, that she was not on sale. This was a woman who would not be bought for a few diamonds or the latest car or a flat in Knightsbridge. Or even all three. Up to this point, Aarav Ruparel had never slept with a woman he had loved because he did not think he could love a woman, not after that moment when he had seen his mother offering love on the cheap in a sordid hotel, dancing for fat businessmen on dream-trips away from their wives and children. And so as soon as he was able, he had turned the women in his life into another commodity. He bought them by offering them much more than they imagined they could ask. He tossed them away when he was done with them but he never turned one down without setting her up in some way: a business to play with, a shop to destroy, a home to rent out, a piece of land to sell. Then it was up to them. Some of his women had turned out to be smart enough to parley their talents into careers. Others had returned to the world of the busy businessman who turned them into a rest stop and had begun the slow march into degradation. Aarav had watched both happen with total detachment.

Once Apoorva had pointed out a once-beautiful red-haired girl from Alsace on the streets of Amsterdam. She had represented a weekend in Paris for Aarav and had got herself a lovely Cartier bracelet out of it. The bracelet was long gone, they both realised, as they saw her trying to beg for money for her next dose of heroin.

'What a state to come to,' Apoorva had said.

Aarav had looked away and shrugged.

'I hate it when you shrug like that,' Apoorva said.

'Why?' Aarav asked.

'Because it makes you look like you don't care.'

'But I don't.'

'That's not a very nice thing to say.'

'Is it nice to pretend to care? Is a lie ever better? For anyone?'

'It may be kinder.'

'I don't want to be kind. I want to be who I am. No, let me put it this way—I want to travel light. And each time you lie, you add something to your baggage. You add something you have to remember. And then you have to add other lies to cover those. Lisette was a lovely moment. She satisfied a need in me and I think I left her happy when I flew out of Charles de Gaulle airport. It was no *grande passion,* not for her and not for me. So do I feel sorry for her now? Yes, I suppose, as much as I feel for anyone who has no control over themselves. No more than I feel for any other woman who is an addict and homeless.'

Apoorva had left well enough alone. He did not know all of what his friend had been through but there were ghosts in those eyes. They were held in control but there were times when they looked out from Aarav's eyes and none of them was pretty.

Aarav stood now at the window of his suite and looked down as a car drew up. Naila got out. He could see she was still talking nineteen to the dozen. And then Vasudha. For a moment, she stood there, and as he looked at her, Aarav made a decision. He picked up the house phone and made a short call.

~

As Vasudha and Naila approached the reception, a young man came up with a message.

'Sir says you must go to Miracle Gardens and he will follow,' he said.

'Chalo then…'

'No, Madam. He says that Ms Prasad will go and he will follow.'

Naila rolled her eyes expressively and said, 'You have my number. When you need anything call me, haan? Because I am your lie…no, what did you say?'

'Liaison. It's a French word.'

'See that? You think you're talking English but you're talking French all the time? This kamabakhat language is a big criminal.'

Vasudha laughed. 'All languages work like that. The word kamra? In Hindi? It comes from Spanish: camera.'

'What you are saying!' Naila exclaimed in English. But she wasn't paying a great deal of attention. The finer points of linguistic cross-pollination were obviously not of much interest. Besides, her phone was ringing and the caller was a big pink heart. 'Uff, this George na? He can't stay without me one minute. You go and see Miracle Garden. Some bigshot Japanese designed it for Ruparel sir.'

Vasudha got back into the car. It was not a long drive; in

fact, they were in the grounds of the hotel still when she got down. It was obviously a Japanese garden. It had all the sparse severity of such a place. The whole thing had been designed as a play of grey and green, the grey of stone against the green of foliage. It was beautiful, but to Vasudha it said nothing.

'Do you like it?' It was Aarav. The man walked on little cat's feet.

'No,' she said, the truth startled out of her.

'Why?'

'A garden is a reminder of all that we are—never perfect, a little untidy, and still somewhat beautiful; always in the process of becoming. But here? Here nature has been tamed forced into shapes and patterns. It's too perfect, too neat. It is man's dominion over nature that is being celebrated, not his dependence on it.'

'Well said,' he said. 'But studies show that Japanese gardens help businessmen relax.'

'Do they? That's probably because it gives them the idea that things can be controlled, even nature.'

He laughed at that, a pleasant sound in the quiet of the garden.

'So what would you do?'

'I would have this garden but I would have another which is a little…untended.'

'Untended?'

'Yes. With a variety of plants, some in leaf, others old and bent. Green leaves, dead leaves… It should be the kind of place where you can come with a small child and not worry about him making a mess. It should have big showy flowers, and no signs that say you can't pick them. It should have lots of swings and benches and carousels. Because a garden with a happy child in it is complete. And this one reminds me of that beautiful Oscar Wilde story of The Selfish Giant.'

'You will have to tell it to me some time.'

'Oh it isn't something that can be told. You have to read it.'

'I don't have time.'

'Then this is your kind of garden.'

'Why do you say that?'

'Because you can look at this garden and take it all in and it will be over in a second. You can label it: Japanese garden. You can grade it: authentic. I think you should have a plaque somewhere that says that Takashi Kitanu designed it. That will help people appreciate it.'

Aarav laughed again.

'Why do you say that?'

'I have noticed that people like to be told that an expert has done something. Then they appreciate it more. If a painting is beautiful, you should be able to enjoy it. But most people want to be told which paintings are the most expensive, which paintings were done by grand masters and they go and look at those.'

'So you don't think it is a good idea?'

'No, I think it is a lovely idea. People like to think that

there is a Japanese garden, just as they like to know there's a sushi bar in the hotel. But when it comes to having a meal they will want a thali too. Put in another garden. It will be your thali garden.'

'Thali garden?' he tried out the words. 'Yes. That's an idea. But this is a business hotel.'

'What an idea that is,' Vasudha sighed. 'It's so strange.'

'Why?'

'I have noticed that businessmen like to think of hotels as if they are places where people come to be something. This hotel is for families. That one is for businessmen. But people are not like that. The businessman who comes with his family to a resort is still a businessman. And even when he comes for a sales conference, he is still a father. I wish we could have hotels that were meant for people and not force-fit people into hotels.'

Aarav looked at her with new respect.

'And in this thali garden, what would you have?'

'I would remind people that we are in the desert.'

'That doesn't sound like such a good idea. Everyone wants to forget about the deserts outside.'

'Yes, they do. But that's because they think of deserts as harsh places. Here, they're not very far from the air-conditioning and the Jacuzzi. Here they will enjoy a desert palm and desert shrubs and thorny cactii. Here they will enjoy eating raw dates. And here the sand will turn them into children again and they will be able to build sandcastles and live their dreams. Here each person can become an Aarav Ruparel.'

'You have five acres and two weeks,' he said. 'I like it. I like the idea of how hard Dubai has worked to erase the desert. And so have we. We have erased the desert and greened it all and now we will erase the greenery and bring back the desert. It will give all those journalists something to talk about.'

'Five acres!' Vasudha threw her arms out and spun around, a child again. Then she hugged Aarav, spontaneously, out of the sheer joy of the creative possibilities that entailed. Almost immediately she pulled away and said, 'Sorry sir!'

He shrugged.

'I'm not. But you may be soon. I have to warn you that I do not spare any member of my team. I believe that we have to work hard. I don't spare myself, either.'

'You have to run very fast to stay where you are, as the Red Queen said to Alice.'

Aarav looked a little confused.

'Didn't you read *Alice in Wonderland* and *Through the Looking-Glass* as a child?'

'My childhood wasn't quite like that,' he said abruptly and turned away.

Two hours after they had gone over some other plans and projects and proposals, he let Vasudha go to her quarters.

~

Vasudha shared the quarters with Naila. On their way, they passed a group of women.

'See those khottis?' Naila said. 'You'll be working with them—some from our Hindustan-Pakistan, some from Sri Lanka, Philippines, Nepal...Dubai is our New York. Come, say hello.' And she called out to the women. 'Hello ladies, babies, scabies. Meet our new friend, fresh from Bombay, Vasudha Prasad.'

Vasudha smiled at them. She liked the faces that smiled back, and felt reassured.

When they reached their quarters, Naila helped Vasudha unpack. 'Hai, what beautiful saris you have. A little too simple, but what's jewellery for! You must let me wear your saris, okay—sometimes, when i want to look sophisticated and all that. Okay?'

'Okay,' Vasudha smiled.

'Oh, and you don't mind, na—I need the light on when I sleep. Otherwise toh I'm terrified. I can't sleep only because I keep thinking—that is one bhoot, this is one pret, oh my Mummy, now a chudail is coming for me, her feet are turned back, her breasts are swaying and they hang to her knees...Eeee! I know, I'm stupid, like a child, but leave the light on, na?'

'No problem,' said Vasudha.

'You are too nice, too much nice,' said Naila. 'Come with me and I will show you something.'

Naila sat Vasudha down at her laptop and gave her her first lesson in Skype.

'And now, who will you see but, ta-da!'

It was Maddy.

'Maddy, how are you, where are you?' Vasudha almost-shouted.

'Gosh, see where-where we've reached and what-what we're doing, no? I'm in Singapore, everything is like Nariman Point, only cleaner, and everyone is Chinese-types. But otherwise, it is so much fun and we are going to Sentosa Island tomorrow.'

'We...?'

And then Saanjh popped up into the screen.

'Maa...'

For a moment, his voice broke and Vasudha had to turn away to mop her eyes. But soon they were both chatting away, oblivious to the man standing just outside the door, looking in, his eyes full of an inscrutable yearning.

~

The sound of Saanjh's young voice saying Maa had brought back Aarav's childhood with a painful rush. It was a childhood in Calcutta. He remembered the warm and happy Anglo-Indian community amongst whom they had lived. They had been kind but feckless, poor but warm. And when they saw a young woman who had a young son to look after, they did not ask too many questions and accepted the stories she told about herself.

Looking back now, Aarav wondered what would have happened if he too had accepted the story she told about herself, that she was a nurse in a hospital and she had to do night shifts because she earned more money that way. But that was not his way. His mind was too sharp, too enquiring.

He had suspected the truth about his mother, long known it somewhere under his skin but he had denied it to himself. She told him she was a nurse and he wanted to believe her but then she couldn't bear the sight of blood. Once he had cut his knee and she had almost fainted. Jeevan Uncle had not been much help either; he had drunk himself into a stupor already. Kind Mrs De Souza from next door had come to his rescue and cleaned his knee. She had muttered that some women didn't deserve the children they had.

'D-up-on't t–up-alk l-up-ike th-up-at,' her husband had said mildly. Of course Aarav knew P-language and understood it immediately.

'Sh-p-e's n-up-o b-up-ett-up-er th-p-an sh-up-e sh-up-ould b-upe,' said Mrs De Souza and gave him a couple of Nice sugar biscuits to eat.

Aarav had asked his teacher in school what it meant if one said someone was no better than they should be and his teacher had looked at him carefully before saying, 'Did someone say that about your mother?'

That evening when his mother went on night shift duty, he had followed her and found that she did not go to a hospital. Instead, it was to a hotel that she went, The Hotel Lucky Start. The S of its illuminated sign was not working and so it now read: Hotel The Lucky tart. His mother walked to the door of a nightclub set into the frontage of the building. A burly man stood there: Tiwari, the guardian of the entry to the underworld.

'Arrey,' he said, 'What are you doing here? This is no place for children.'

'Nothing,' Aarav said. 'My mother works here.'

'Nice mother you have,' the man said.

'Maa forgot her purse. I brought it for her.'

'Achha?' The man was not convinced but Aarav had prepared his story well and he took from his schoolbag his mother's second-best handbag, the one she used when she was going out with Jeevan Uncle. That was not very often because Jeevan Uncle was seldom in a state to do much going out or coming in. He slipped past the man at the door now and walked into the club. It was cold inside, air-conditioning licking at his body. The air was thick with the smell of smoke and alcohol and pickled onions. And there on a stage, in a spotlight, stood his mother. She was not wearing the dress she had worn when she left home; she was now in a long red gown and long gloves. She looked quite beautiful as she stood there, swaying and singing. For just a moment his heart filled with pride at how lovely she looked, and how...

Then the dream had been ripped open and he had begun to bleed.

'Hoy,' shouted a man in the audience. 'Are you going to stand there all night or are you going to dance?'

And his mother threw back her head, exposing the slim column of her slender neck, and laughed. It was a sound that was balanced somewhere between laughter and tears. The music picked up tempo and she began to shake her booty.

Then she turned her back on the audience and looked over her shoulder at them.

'Should I go?' she mocked them.

'No,' shouted the men, some adding suggestions about things she could do to make them happy. Most of these involved her taking off her clothes.

'Like this?' she asked and slowly peeled a glove off her hand and then dangled it at the audience which responded with a medley of hoots and whistles.

She turned to look over her other shoulder and then reached for the other glove…and suddenly she saw her son, standing there, looking at her, his eyes full of hurt, his heart full of betrayal.

Then he turned and ran.

~

He had been running ever since, he realised, as he stood outside the circle of love represented by Vasudha and her son. He could feel the intense emotions that underlay what they were saying even as they exchanged banalities about the weather and what Saanjh had eaten and whether he had brushed his teeth and washed his hands, between his fingers…

'Show me your finger nails,' Vasudha was ordering now. The screen filled up with two young hands, palms downwards.

'Good. Thank you Maddy.'

'Hey, all your training, Vasu. Even I'm learning—sing

Happy Birthday song first verse two times when washing hands and rub between the fingers and rub the nails and whoknowswhat. My whole day will go now in washing the hands. So I didn't do nothing.'

'Didn't do *anything*,' Vasudha corrected her.

'Hai, I don't know who is going to correct my English now that you're gone.'

'We can chat on Skype,' said Vasudha.

'Chal, let's see, I'll have to get one laptop for home use and then who will let me sit?' Maddy sighed.

Aarav was filled with a sudden need to speak to his own mother. He went back to his room, another hotel room, and dialled her number. Her familiar voice filled the room.

'Are you well?'

He picked up a pad that lay by the bedside and began to doodle.

'Yeah, Maa. You?'

'If you ask an old woman that, she's likely to tell you how she is and the rest of your day will go in discussions about bowel movements and falls...'

'Did you fall, Ma?'

'No, no, I'm just using that as an example.'

'Well don't. Haven't you heard, shubh shubh bolo?'

'Just in case a passing angel might hear and say 'Tathasthu'? I have my angel on the phone with me right now. I have only to express a wish and it materialises. So I'm not really going to let myself worry about that one.'

There was a moment's silence. Then his mother, wise to his ways, asked, 'What is it?'

'Nothing, Maa. Just felt like hearing your voice.'

'That is nice. What is her name?'

'Vasudha,' he said, because his guard was down and he was drawing her name on the pad in front of him.

'Ah good,' said his mother. 'I am so happy for you.'

'Maa, it's not like that.'

'No, it is never the same way. It is never the same way inside one heart. It can happen several times and each time will be different. How could it be 'like that'? There is no 'like that'.'

'Who's talking about love?'

'No one. I didn't mention it, did I?'

He thought back. No, she hadn't mentioned it. He had. Tricked again. He laughed and in another country, another time zone, his mother relished the sound. He sounded alive and vibrant with energy. Not just the acquisitive energy that money brought with it and the ability to buy things. This was the sound of a man in love and enjoying it.

'There's a problem, Maa,' he said now.

'There is always a problem,' she countered. 'Don't let that worry you. Don't let it take away the sweetness of the moment. Face the problem and see what you can do about it.'

'I feel like the King of Lanka. I have the lady in my power but I may not touch her.'

'She's married?'

'She is. There's a kid too.'

His mother sighed. The good ones had always been

married, in her experience. That had never prevented love from forcing its way through.

'The husband?'

'He seems to be missing. In more ways than one. I think she said he's wanted by the police.'

'That doesn't sound like much of a Purushottam to me,' she sighed, 'and sometimes the lady will love against her will. And sometimes the lady must find her way out of a maze of loyalty and tradition, the feeling that something is owed.'

'Is it? Is it owed?'

'I don't know. I can't answer that. I know I owe your father for you but he owes me for so much else. For support and for being there. For sharing you in your sickness and sharing you in your joys. I don't know how to balance one against the other. One day, I think: whatever else he did, he gave me Aarav. One day I think: what a fool he is to have walked away from us. A third day, I think: how did I manage? And I did manage, didn't I?'

His heart sprang a leak.

'We came through, Maa. We came through. It doesn't matter what we went through, we came through.'

'That's the spirit. You'll come through. If she's tough and she's been abandoned by her husband and has a kid and is still standing...'

'...and how!'

'Then she has had no option but to be tough. So she will come through too. And then you may find a space where you can be together.'

'What can I do, Maa?'

'You can turn yourself into a woman. Because men think they must always *do* things. And there is sometimes nothing you can do but wait. Do you remember how I once took you to Easter service?'

'Yes, it was beautiful, the whole church dark, the candles then lighting each other up, one by one...'

'But do you remember what you said?'

He did.

The priest's sermon that day had been about the faithfulness of women. He had pointed out that Christ had asked his male followers to stay awake with Him, to pray with Him and help Him get through the fearful night that preceded the crucifixion. And they had slept. He had come to find them asleep and had cried out to them. But they had slept again.

'And now I turn,' the priest said, 'to the figure of Stabat Mater, the mother standing by the cross. She cannot do anything. She cannot intervene. She cannot console her son nor can she turn his terrible fate away. But she can be there. She can wait. She can be present. And this is what she does. She waits. She stands. She gives witness. If Christ had asked his female followers to wait—and He had many of them—he would have found the comfort He sought in the Garden of Gethsemane.'

Now his mother's voice came to him, filtered by technology but still mint-cool.

'You must wait. Do you remember that poem I once

read to you? About how the poet, the lover and the birdwatcher must be patient?'

Poetry, Aarav thought, as he bade his mother goodnight and prepared to sleep, had a strange power of consolation. It was as if a stranger reached out and consoled you in a moment of grief that you did not even know you were experiencing.

SEVEN

Two weeks later, the air on Aarav's morning run had turned crisp. The weather was changing, he thought, and it was a pity that he was leaving for Switzerland just when it would get mild and pleasant in Dubai, even if only for brief periods.

He had a shower and an egg-white omelette for breakfast and then Apoorva arrived.

'Passport?'

'Check.'

'Credit cards?'

'Check.'

'Money?'

'In six currencies including dollars.'

Aarav was the only billionaire who ever bothered with money. Most of the others Apoorva knew worked in worlds that were driven by plastic. Or they had their assistants to hand out cash when it was needed. Aarav did not believe in outsourcing payments. He ran his own ship and Apoorva knew that Aarav would be able to account for every last dollar when the trip ended.

'Laptop?'

'Check. iPhone. Check.'

In truth, he did not need Apoorva to go over all this with him but it was a ritual they had formed several years ago and it was not an easy one to break. Aarav thought of it as Apoorva's way of showing his concern.

Or love. Why, he wondered, did it seem so difficult to talk about love? Was it because he didn't believe in it? That was stupid, he told himself, because the world offered, again and again, instances of love, not just love that was mentioned or spoken of but love in action. There were parents who sacrificed their lives to children. There were monks who sacrificed their lives for the good of humanity. There were teachers who worked for students and doctors in remote areas, working under fire, saving lives, not because they cared for some person but out of a disinterested love of humanity. There were young women who killed themselves because of love and young men who killed because of love. And vice versa. No, only a cynic could doubt the power of love or its reality; and only a fool could be a cynic.

He scooped up the last piece of multi-grain toast and spread it with a little of the premium conserve that came from Mount Athos in Greece. Then he stepped out of his suite and as he turned to speak to Apoorva, a white design caught his eye.

He looked down. It was a design done in rice flour, a rangoli. He remembered his mother making them when she remembered. He had often had to remind her about Diwali. Was it…?

He walked down the corridor and found that every room had a rangoli outside it, even though the rooms were empty. The rangoli designs led in a trail down the stairs and into the front lobby where the finishing touches were being put on a giant rangoli of a myriad colours and of almost fractal-like complicatedness. There were seven or eight women working on it.

In the middle was Vasudha.

'What is this?' he asked.

Vasudha turned and looked at him, her eyes alight.

'It's Diwali tomorrow, sir. So many of us are far from home, I thought it might be nice if we could celebrate it.'

'It is actually quite an idea.'

'It might not work everywhere,' said Apoorva diplomatically. Aarav nodded.

'But here, now, and when the hotel isn't opened? It's lovely.'

'I'd like a picture of it for the company magazine,' he said.

There was a scurrying and a flurrying and several cameras were considered and rejected and finally a Lumia was produced and Aarav smiled as a suitable angle was judged. It took much less time than it would have normally taken but the staff were already quite accustomed to the idea that they should be ready to move at a minute's notice and deliver the goods in the next ten seconds after that. It was the Aarav Ruparel style.

'Now, I'd like a photograph with the person whose idea it was,' he said and handed over his own iPad.

There was a moment of total silence and then everyone exhaled a long breath. Vasudha flushed and went pale.

'Also for the magazine,' said Aarav silkily.

Naila came forward and pulled out a compact from her bag, getting ready to dust Vasudha's nose with some powder.

'No need to gild the lily,' Aarav said and took his position next to her.

Vasudha straightened her back and then adjusted her sari pallu so that her mangalsutra was clearly visible. The photograph was taken and Aarav smiled and turned to the exit.

'Won't you be here, sir?' Vasudha asked.

'I will be in Switzerland,' he said. 'Buying six chalets to set up a chain of boutique hotels. The fine print on the deal.'

In the car, Apoorva looked a little grim.

'What happened?' said Aarav.

'It's not like you to tell the new hire what you're planning to do,' he said. 'Normally, you wouldn't even say where you're going.'

'I don't think anyone asked before.'

'I don't think anyone dared.'

'Well there you are then. I might even have told people where I was going and what I was planning if someone had dared.'

Apoorva wanted to point out that Vasudha had not asked. Aarav had volunteered the information, on his own.

'You do remember that she's married and that she's married to some highly unsavoury type.'

Aarav smiled but it was a bleak smile: 'I am reminded each time I see the mangalsutra around her neck,' he said.

Back in the hotel, Naila was giggling.

'Ooh, he wanted a photo with you, haan? Too much,' she said as they went together to clean out the suite Aarav had occupied. This job would generally have been assigned to staff at much lower segments of the hierarchy but when the boss comes and goes, it is best for the senior management to make sure that everything is as it should be. Because it is not the juniors who will take the firing.

'Don't be silly, Naila,' said Vasudha but she could not help hoping that Aarav had not meant that picture for the office magazine. She wished she had a picture of him…and then she squashed the thought. What need, she asked herself, when his face floated in front of her eyes every time she closed them. It was not a handsome face, she had to say, but there was a certain energy in it, a vitality that more than compensated for any lack of symmetry. Aarav Ruparel had the ability to exude command; when he walked into a room, he owned it. You could not stop looking at him; there was something about him that warned you that to take your eyes off him might be costly.

Vasudha and Naila entered the room together and began to go through the motions of checking what had been used, what needed to be changed, what had to be refreshed. Naila stopped by the stationery at the side of the bed and said, 'Aai-haai!' in a tone that was better suited to a pubescent girl in a boarding school. She looked at Vasudha and began to simper coyly.

'What is it?' Vasudha asked.

'Oh oh oh oh, mujhe kisise pyaar ho gaya,' Naila sang and began to dance around the room, holding up the writing pad that lay next to the telephone.

'Show me that!'

Naila made a great show of fanning herself as if she were overheating.

'Saawan agan lagaaye to usse kaun bhujaaye?' she sang now and danced away from Vasudha.

'Don't be silly, Naila,' said Vasudha. 'Show it to me.'

'Yeh mera deewaanapan hai ya mohabbat ka...'

But then Vasudha grabbed her and dragged her arm down.

'Uff, nigodiye,' said Naila. 'You're doing so much zulm. And all I am doing is celebrating your new love.'

Vasudha finally laid hands on the paper and there in Aarav's unmistakable handwriting was her name, written again and again.

EIGHT

The day of his return from Switzerland, Aarav was tired. The sale of the chalets had gone well, exceptionally well. They had signed the deal in record time.

'Should we be buying now?' Apoorva asked him on the flight to Dubai.

'No time like this,' Aarav replied. 'This is when prices will be really low and for a few million dollars we can acquire stakes in some lovely properties.'

'But no one wants to travel these days. They don't want to take flights because now some people have taken to shooting down planes and sometimes you don't even find the wreckage. They don't want to go to Africa because they might end up with some disease that looks like it belongs in a Hollywood horror movie. They don't want to go to India because they think we rape women on buses and in deserted mills and in parking lots. They don't want to go to the beaches because of the fear of tsunamis and typhoons. I think everyone wants to stay at home now.'

'Yes, they do. But that will pass. They will want to travel again. That's human nature.'

'You mean they want to boast that they've been there, done that, got the t-shirt?'

'That's part of it, yes. But it's not the only part of it. I think it's got to do with our hunter-gatherer instinct. Look how far we've ranged. There are men in the most inhospitable deserts. There are men on the coldest of Arctic floes. There are men where it gets to fifty degrees in the summer and in places where it rains for months at a time. Travel is in our genes. It's what makes us human, this feeling that over the next hill, past the familiar sights, there will be something new and exciting that I should not miss. And when they do want to travel again, we'll be there for them, with something bigger and better.'

'With a growing plant in every room?'

'Indeed, yes,' said Aarav and in order to forestall the lecture he knew was coming, he closed his eyes and reclined his seat and pretended to go to sleep. All he wanted to do was relish the thought that he was going to see Vasudha soon. Apoorva knew him too well to be fooled. He knew this was a ploy and so he simply changed the topic.

'Next stop, Kolkata?' Apoorva said.

Aarav opened his eyes. That was one subject that always got his attention.

'Has it all been set up?'

'Everything in place. The hotel is sinking rapidly. With the new government in power in Bengal, what little money they managed to attract has skipped it to other states. The lady's not for turning, it is said. And The Lucky Start…'

'The Lucky Tart,' Aarav said to himself.

'…has positioned itself as a business hotel. I suppose they were hoping that with the Commies gone, money would start pouring in and it would be like the good old days…'

'Good old days? Those date back to the time when jute was the only packing material and the capital of the British Empire was in Calcutta.'

'What can I say?' Apoorva said. 'Memories are long in Bengal.'

That startled a chuckle out of Apoorva.

'What are they asking?'

'Seventeen.'

'Your take?'

'Over-priced. You can have it for ten.'

'Why?'

'Debt. Sujoy Bose will own the hotel for another three or four months, max, depending on how many of the bhadralok he can wine and dine and then beg for another extension. But the banks are now restless. They want to see returns or repayments or they want another asset.'

'The Tart would be an asset?'

'You know what Conrad Hilton said? Location, location, location. It's a beautiful address. It's got all these old Art

Deco fittings. I've heard that the staff have started taking old taps and switches and that kind of thing home to sell to dealers. No, don't look like that. Salaries have been delayed too. The Lucky Start is just waiting to fall into your lap.'

Aarav smiled.

'I have one question,' said Apoorva.

'What?'

'Why this hotel?'

'Why not?'

'That's never a very good answer.'

'Is seventeen crores going to hurt us?'

'You know to the last paisa what you have. You know that you could buy it out of your personal earnings. Or your bonus last year.'

'That's a thought.'

'No, I would not advise...'

'Don't worry. I'm not going to break all my traditions at once. This will be one of the chain.'

'But you do know...'

'I know that even a dead elephant is a good deal of money. There's money to be made there. I want it turned into a colonial club where all those who have been turned away by the colonial clubs for not having the right accent or the right education can come and be treated as if they were bhadralok. I don't want this for its future, I want it for its past. We're going to dig out every single old stick of furniture, every starched bandgala, every old piece of China we can find and we're going to play make-believe. We're going to play British Raj with brown-skinned sahibs.'

'It might work.'

'Oh it will work all right. I will dream it up. Vasudha will understand it. You will execute it.'

Vasudha. That name again. Apoorva frowned.

The cabin attendant came up.

'Sir, we are about to land.'

'No,' said Aarav, 'we're about to take off.'

~

Vasudha walked through the rows and rows of desert roses that she had selected as the theme for the rooms of the Noor.

'You look like small light bulbs,' she said to the plants. 'You feel like the desert. You will live in these rooms and you will work for us, as plants always have. Where would we be without your ability to turn energy into food? You turn your green palms towards the sun and draw its strength down into your depths and then along comes an animal, maybe a goat or a buffalo or a deer or even a man, and eats you and you enter into us. You make us who we are and for this we offer you our thanks. In your strength lies our beauty. In your beauty lies our strength.'

'That was beautiful. Again.'

Vasudha spun around. Aarav was standing behind her.

'What you just said? I want you to say it again.'

'I don't know that I can.'

'Please.'

His voice was a command. She raised an eyebrow.

'Please,' he modified it but the arrogance was still there. He had no idea that he was being arrogant. He had not really asked for anything in his life.

'Please,' he said now but he was looking at her lips and he was a little closer than he had been. The air was charged. It must be all the oxygen the plants were releasing. That was why she felt dizzy now, no, not dizzy, light-headed, as if she were a sodawater bottle, fizzing and popping.

'Aarav?'

It was Apoorva.

'I want you to write down what you said and put in on a small card next to each living plant in each hotel room all over the country. And it will carry your name.'

'The flight to Kolkata will leave.'

'I must go.'

'Miles to go before I sleep,' she said. He looked startled, as if she were prescient.

'And promises to keep, yes,' he nodded his head.

'Good luck,' she said and his face hardened.

'I don't believe in luck. If I did, I should still be in a slum in a city with no hope.'

She looked at him and saw a little boy who must have had it tough growing up. Perhaps he had been like Saanjh, wanting to defend someone against the adult world. Perhaps that was what had toughened him to the point where he looked upon the world as an adversary and the next deal as a battle.

'Temper justice with mercy,' she said.

'What?' he said but she was hurrying away.

~

The smell of the city had not changed. Nor had the taxis that trundled about, yellow beetles that looked like they were badly in need of retirement. Aarav made a mental note to stop for a roll at New Market and to see whether jhaalmuri was on the menu at The Lucky Tart. It could be had in the streets, of course, but nothing seduced people with money to spend on street food turned into a hygienic dish by cooks who wore gloves and tucked their hair into caps.

He looked down at the pad by his side and was about to make a note when he noticed that he had already made several. But they were all the same: one name, Vasudha.

There was a connection there. How had she known he was going to act without mercy? It was as if she could read his mind.

It was time to own up, he thought.

But first he had some unfinished business with a man named Sujoy Bose.

~

The years had not dealt kindly with Sujoy Bose. Where he had once been a sleek young man who held the fates of his employees in the whimsical palm of his hand, he was now a whiskey-bloated man with a comb-over that couldn't disguise his baldness.

'You have come to the wrong place,' he said.

'Indeed?' Apoorva said.

'Tell Aarav Babu that I will not sell my hotel.'

'No?'

'Tell him that it has been in my family for three generations. My grandfather bought the land. My father built the hotel.'

'And you ran it into the ground,' said Apoorva.

'Apoorva saaheb, you should know how business is. You go through bad patches. But the business is sound and I have much goodwill in the market.'

He caught Aarav's eyes on him. He tried to smile but met with no response. Apoorva logged on to Thorntree on his phone.

'This goodwill. Here's someone who stayed here a week ago: "Broke my heart going back to The Lucky Start,"' he read aloud. 'Today's comment: "The old place is a ghost of itself. They hadn't changed the towels before I entered the room. I found a lipstick stain on one." And here's a nice one: "It may have had a lucky start but it's not going to be much of a lucky finish."'

'Ori-baba, now you're going to believe every lie that Indian travellers write? You know the kind, na? They take the smallest room and rob everything they can from the toiletries to the towels and then they think they can badmouth us,' said Sujoy Bose. Aarav continued to stare at him.

'People can lie. Clients can lie. But numbers don't,'

said Apoorva. 'Your time is up, Mr Bose. We can do this two ways. We can do it the hard way or we can do it the Aarav Ruparel way.'

'Oh the Aarav Ruparel way is the nice way, is it?'

Apoorva was about to reply when Aarav spoke.

'Mr Sujoy Bose, I could go to the banks right now and buy your hotel from under you, land and grandfather and all. Instead, I have come to you with an offer of eighteen crores.'

Apoorva made a sound of disgust.

'Eighteen crores for a lifetime of emotions…'

'You wouldn't know an emotion if it came up and bit your hindquarters,' Aarav said. 'But if you want I can buy off your debt from the bank and then come after you with it. I can get this hotel stripped and sold, bit by bit, and I can take you and your family and throw them on the roads. I would love to see that happen.'

'This sounds like a personal vendetta,' said Sujoy.

'It is,' said Aarav, 'It is personal. Make no mistake. I would love to see you and your family begging in Park Lane. So I would advise you to sign, seal and deliver the contracts in the case…'

He looked over his shoulder. Apoorva took out the case.

'I would love to destroy you but I have been told to temper justice with mercy.'

Apoorva gave another snort.

'But make one small squeak of protest and you will have

run out of chances and choices. I will grind you under my heel. Personally.'

Then he turned and walked out. He had waited for this moment for so many years. Now it was here. Why did he feel hollow?

As he got into the car, he saw that the papers were reporting a flood in Orissa.

'Let's sell the hotel again,' he said. 'And give the money to flood relief.'

~

'Three meetings in Singapore and then we go to Australia. The Pacific Rim...'

'Cancel them.'

'What?' Apoorva was aghast.

'We're going back to Dubai.'

'Why?'

'The why is in Dubai.'

'This is going too far.'

Aarav turned to his friend and his eyes were honest and grave.

'This has not gone far enough.'

'She's a married woman. She has a son.'

'I like the idea of a ready-made family.'

'You want to...'

'I have said too much already. This is a conversation I should be having with her.'

This time he did not need to pretend sleep. Apoorva

needed time to assess the situation and so he shut his mouth and stared steadily out of the window. After a few minutes of thought, he began to investigate 'divorce laws, India' on the Internet.

~

The number was a Mumbai number. Had something happened to the old lady? Vasudha wondered as she answered.

It was Patil.

'So you have left the country?'

'How did you get this number?'

'We are the police, madam. We can get pretty much any number we want. And when it's a matter of national interest…'

'How can I be of national interest?'

'You are not. Your husband is. And as you seem to be the only person who can lead us to him, you're now on our radar.'

Hari. Hari. Hari. It was as if she would never be free of him. He had had his name tattooed on her body and it seemed as if the ink had spilled from there into their fates, conjoining them forever. However far she went, however hard she ran, however much she worked, Hari would follow her. At some level, she knew she had no way of avoiding this. Because Saanjh was half his genetic material too. Saanjh united the two of them in his small person. But this spilling was more than she could take.

She simply hung up. The phone rang again. She picked it up and said, 'Look Mr Patil, I don't think you understand something simple...'

'Hello, what Patil-Shatil? This is George. Can I talk to Naila?'

Vasudha covered the receiver and called Naila.

'Ooh Georgie Porgey, you've come to kiss this girl and make her cry or what?' Naila cooed. Vasudha turned to look out of the window. The sky was an unusual colour, as if the desert had risen up to meet it. A sandstorm was brewing, unusual for this time of year.

The conversation behind her followed the usual pattern that left her deeply uncomfortable.

'Arrey my Georgie Porgie, I'm coming, baby, as soon as I get off work...but listen, not that construction workers' hotel again, okay? Spend some money on me, yaar, take me to Hyat-Shyat...Sending all your money to that bhains in Goa. She's your wife, I'm your life...'

As Naila turned ordinary conversational gambits—'How can you ask if I'm coming, you dirty boy?'—into sexual innuendoes, Vasudha's face hardened. When Naila was done with the usual quantity of smacking farewell kisses, she said, 'Naila, I wish you wouldn't.'

And as soon as she said it, she wondered what had made her do this. Outside the storm began to rage. It scraped its sandpaper tongue against the buildings. The trees did not even try to withstand its rage. They simply allowed themselves to be bent and whipped around.

'Wouldn't what?' Naila turned and looked at her, a challenge in her eyes.

The streets emptied. The traffic slowed to a crawl.

'I wish you wouldn't conduct your extramarital affair in such a blatant fashion.'

'At least I do it without pretence.'

'Pretence?'

'Yes, my dear, pretence. There's a certain man in this company who hires you though you don't have an education. He gives you a job and he brings you to Dubai. He pays for your son to go to a Singapore school. He writes your names on chits of paper and he treats every word you say as if it were coming from the President of America. And you want everyone to believe that there's nothing going on?'

'Naila, I have never…we have never…'

'Uff, meri paak-daaman. You have done nothing, you have only had some thoughts that you are deeply ashamed of. That's the problem, isn't it? Okay, you choose your way and I will choose mine. You do what you feel is good for you and I will do what I think is good for me. No, you're not a hypocrite, and yes, I'm a slut. Happy? Now go and tell your 'boss' that I'm a bad woman and he should sack me and I will collect my things and go.'

She turned and walked out of the room, leaving Vasudha devastated. Was she truly a hypocrite to wear a mangalsutra when she loved another man? What sense did it make to say that one was married and that one was married for life—no, for seven lifetimes—to a man one had not chosen and whom one had never loved? If they were half each other, she was his ardhangini, half his body, what did it mean that he had lived with her for only a few months before vanishing? But there was something in her that clung to the way things were, that needed the security of the relationship. And in this she saw her dilemma: it was not about Aarav. It was not about Hari. It was not even about Saanjh, however impossible it was to imagine a situation now that did not involve taking him and his interests into consideration. It was about Vasudha herself. It was about how she saw herself and how she saw her life.

She looked around at her surroundings. They had nothing of hers, except for a small potted plant. She sat down and pulled up a notepad towards her and wrote a note for Naila. Then she picked up the plant and plunged out of the room, running down the stairs.

~

The air was thick with a storm when their flight landed.

'We should wait this out,' Apoorva said.

'I've done enough waiting,' said Aarav and walked out of the airport.

'Sir,' said the chauffeur that the hotel had sent for them, 'It is not safe for me to drive.'

'Perhaps. Give me the keys.'

It was a long time since he had thrown himself against a storm. It ripped at his hair and skin for the few moments he was exposed, before he fitted himself into the car and enclosed himself in its metallic skin. Few people who had not been caught in the storm were braving the roads. Some had simply steered their cars to the side of the highway and parked, hunkering down and waiting so that the fury of nature might get some time to abate or choose another target. That meant Aarav had a clear drive, just so long as the Mercedes' engine held true and a small speck of dust did not get into one of the many computers that it now took to get from Point A to Point B. Aarav realised that he might want to think of this as a war between him and the elements but all he had to do was hold on to the steering wheel—and it took some effort to do that as the car bucked and turned the wheel in his hands, forcing him to use all the power of his steely wrists and forearms—but this was a struggle between the elements and the idea of a machine.

He did not realise how much he had been sweating until he jumped out of the car at the staff quarters. It was exactly at this moment that Naila emerged from the lift doors. She saw Aarav and she saw the storm outside and she made up her mind: a sensible woman would not brave all of this. She would, she thought, take her chops and she stepped back into the lift and pressed the button for her floor.

'Is she there?' Aarav asked as they began the ascent.

'She was when I left,' said Naila.

Aarav took in her flushed cheeks and said, 'You had an argument?'

'Who can have an argument with Vasudha?' asked Naila. 'There is no topic on which you can argue with her.' And then because Naila was congenitally unable to leave well enough alone, she said, 'Except on the subject of you.'

He turned his laser eyes on her, sharp, assessing, but then he smiled.

'That's reassuring,' he said.

When they opened the door to the flat, however, Vasudha was gone. There was a note. Naila read it quickly and stuck her tongue out in shame. Aarav took it from her and read it.

> Dear Naila,
>
> In the eyes of a friend, you may see the truth of your life. You were right in what you said about me even if I may still not believe that yours is a good way to be. I must get out of here now before I turn the thought into the deed. And to me, in the real world, the deed is always going to be more of a sin than the thought, even if I know that few might agree.
>
> With my apologies,
> Vasudha

NINE

He found her in the garden, the one she had planned for families to cut loose and enjoy themselves. All around them was the quiet devastation of the dream.

He went and sat down beside her but he did not touch her. His entire body wanted to reach out to her. He wanted to comfort her but he knew that at this moment, she was not to be touched.

'You are running from the truth,' he said.

'I know,' she said, hollowly.

'You are married. I know that. You are married in body and mind. I know that. But you are in love with me. I know that...' he gestured when she tried to protest, 'I love you too. You know that. Somewhere, in some way, we have said this to each other already.'

She looked at him.

'Can you not see that even if you don't say it in words, if you say it with who you are, it is more elemental than anything the world decides? Can you not see that it is your spirit that has spoken to mine?'

'I don't even know who you are,' she said.

He smiled.

'It is not a story that is easy to tell. When I look back, I see how little it might have taken to swing things the other way. How hard luck and drive and skill and stubbornness are all very well, but sometimes the gods must also take a hand in things. Like the day my mother stopped working as a dancer in a bar, taking off her clothes to feed her son and her lover.'

Vasudha felt the words descend like blows.

'Don't worry. You will, I hope, one day meet my mother. You will see that she has survived all that. Tell me, Vasudha, what is more intimate, what is more important, what is more essentially us—the products of the body or the products of the mind?'

'The products of the mind, of course.'

'And yet our society asks us to sell the products of our mind. We respect those who do. Those who sell their bodies, whether as organ donors or as prostitutes, they earn our scorn. How is that?'

'It is the way the world is organised.'

'And it was once the way the world was organised that when a man married a woman, they became one. Their bodies and their souls, yes, but her property too. It was once the way the world was organised that you could buy another human being, body and mind and soul and even the children of her body. The world has rules but it makes and remakes them. My mother did what she could to keep us going.'

Vasudha looked at him and felt her heart go mournful at what the boy must have gone through, what it must have cost him to devise this logical defence of his world.

'You're right,' she said. 'But it isn't only logic that runs the world. You say this land is yours. Because you bought it. Who sold it to you? How did he have the right to sell it? Who gave it to him in the first place? Where did the idea that land might be owned by some people and others kept away from it begin? How do we in India, who believe that the world is our family, Vasudaivam kutmbakam, practice caste? How is it that everyone agrees there is one God and then goes to battle to defend one faith over all others?'

'Vasudha, we could argue these things forever. There is no logic in most of what we do. We feel and do things because of who we are—our imaginations, our histories, our stories. I want you to understand my feelings, my imagination. Understand my story. And then you will be free to choose what to do.'

Now Aarav was beginning to drift through time and space, back to The Lucky Start where he and Jeevan Uncle were waiting for Rohini. He did not know what was going on inside.

Rohini, his mother, had been in the habit of stealing food and drink, food for her son, drink for her lover. She would fill bottles with whatever was left over from glasses, concocting a deeply intoxicating cocktail of a hundred different alcohols and mixers. And she would take an egg or two, a slice of bread, a small bunch of grapes…whatever she thought would not be missed.

Tiwari had noticed that her bag would get a little larger when she was leaving, a little heavier. He had gone and talked to Sujoy Bose about it. Today, they were both waiting for her.

'Off now?' Bose asked.

'Yes,' said Rohini. The hours were long and trying to keep a look of seductive enjoyment on her face was getting to be a greater and greater strain. Sometimes she had no energy to even smile at the end of her shift.

'Your bag looks heavy. Let me help you with it,' Bose said.

'I'll manage thank you.'

'You'll manage? If your bag gets any heavier, it might break your shoulder.'

'Please…'

But Tiwari was already moving towards her. Rohini knew that she was cornered and the graceful thing to do would be to hand over the bag and shrug and apologise and go home empty-handed. But after working all night at a job that sapped her soul of its strength, her mind did the opposite.

'Touch my bag, go on, I dare you!' she challenged them.

Whose voice was that shrill with rage? Who was shouting

as if she were a fishwife in a market? Her own? Surely not? She noticed dully, as if from a distance, that Bose and Tiwari were also changing. They had looked earlier like bullies on a school playground, out for a little fun at the expense of someone weak and defenceless. But now their faces took on the sullenness of the affronted male ego.

'Chudail, how dare you talk to the boss like that?' Tiwari shouted and grabbed her bag. The old and shabby thing burst open and her sad loot fell on the floor.

'Thief. Liar. Shameless hussy!' Bose shouted.

'Don't you dare talk to me like that,' she shouted back. Now she was aware that she had burned her boats. There was no going back.

'The first I heard of all this,' Aarav told Vasudha as they sat in the storm-ravaged remnants of a dream garden, 'was when they threw my mother out on the street that night and Tiwari, the security guard, slammed the door on her. When I heard what had happened, in my heart I was glad. She could not go back there. She would not do that job again. She looked up at Jeevan Uncle. I don't know what happened to him in that moment, what was said without words, but he helped her up and wiped her tears away gently and took her in his arms and walked us all home. Then when he had put her to bed and I went to make tea for us, he said, 'I'm going out. I won't be long.' The next thing I knew a policeman had turned up at the doorstep to tell us that Jeevan Uncle was in hospital. He had thrown himself under the wheels of a tram.'

'Devi ma,' murmured Vasudha under her breath.

'Do you know why I was in Kolkata yesterday? I went there to buy The Lucky Start?'

'The hotel in which she danced?'

'The hotel in which she danced. And who should I see at the gate but Tiwari. I thought: what did you do to me? To her? And in that instant, I heard your voice telling me to temper justice with mercy.'

'Your face was so hard that day when you were leaving. You looked like an avenging angel,' said Vasudha.

'I was. I went there with a mind to grind that Tiwari, that Sujoy to dust. And I saw men who had forced me to grow up. There are thousands of men in India who live off the work of women. No, I think, most Indian men live off the work of women, except for a few city-dwellers. I too had been living off my mother's earnings. By getting her thrown out of the job, Tiwari had forced me to grow up. Standing on the street that day, I felt her sorrow and humiliation so deeply. I had been called everything, randi ka beta, kulta ka ladka, and it had hurt but I had borne the hurt and fought or laughed but I had done nothing to change that reality. Tiwari was different. He hit me where it hurt the most. He hit me where I was vulnerable. He hit someone I loved. He humiliated her and he laid the foundation stone for my success, for everything I have now. On the pavement that day, I promised myself that I would provide, that it was my duty to provide for all those I love. And so whether you leave today or you stay, I will make sure you are provided for, because I love you.'

'Will you buy my love?' Vasudha asked but there was no anger in her voice, only empathy.

'In all these years, among all these women, I have discovered that there is no buying love. You can buy pleasure and you can buy lies. But you cannot buy what we have, Vasudha. Nor can I even begin to hope to repay you for the richness you have brought into my life. It is as if I had been sleeping in sandpaper all my life and suddenly that has been transformed into silk.'

'Cotton. It is much better to sleep on cotton.'

Aarav began to laugh.

'Do you have any idea how much I love you?' he asked as if it were the most natural question in the world. 'And most of all because I can never guess what you're going to say.'

Suddenly Vasudha knew where she belonged. She put her arms around the man she loved and thanked Naila in her heart.

They sat together for a long time and when they rose to leave, Aarav picked up the potted plant that Vasudha had brought with her. He began to dig in the ground and together they planted the little plant out in the air and the sun. Another storm might come and it might die but there was always green, always the green that came crawling back.

~

'Where are you taking me?' Vasudha asked. They were sitting in another airplane and it seemed as if they were headed to India.

'I want you to see the end of the story I began to tell you yesterday,' he said. 'I don't think I can tell you that. I will have to show it to you.'

Vasudha smiled. She had found herself doing a lot in the last few hours. That morning, she had woken with a song in her heart, After her bath, she had dressed and as the last stage of that, she would always slip her mangalsutra over her head. That morning she had hesitated and finally left it there. She was about to leave when she realised she could not and had rushed back to pick it up. But equally she could not put it around her neck, and so she had slipped it into her handbag.

She wondered now if Aarav had noticed.

Aarav had noticed and when Apoorva had given him the number of the best divorce lawyer in Mumbai, he had merely nodded.

'Thank you, Apu,' he had said and his voice had reflected his gratitude. Apoorva had looked at him and decided not to continue with what he had planned to say.

When they arrived at Chennai airport, Vasudha was sleeping, her head nestled on Aarav's arm. When they drove through the verdant countryside of the coast, heading into the Velliangiri hills, he was asleep on her shoulder. Finally the car drew up outside a lovely old bungalow in the colonial style. Huge frangipani trees framed it and bougainvillea threw up excited arms of greeting. A kingfisher's iridescent blue caught Vasudha's eye.

'Come,' he said but already the doors were being thrown

open and a woman was rushing out. She threw her arms around Aarav and tried to say something but then contented herself with dragging his face down and raining kisses on it. Then she saw Vasudha standing behind him.

'Ah,' she said. 'You have brought her.'

'I have.'

'Is she the one?'

'She is.'

'Does she know it?'

'You should ask her.'

Rohini let go of her son and walked to Vasudha. She scanned the younger woman's face with care, as if hoping to find something there. Vasudha met her eyes for a long time and then looked away.

Rohini sighed.

'You go and freshen up,' she said to Aarav, 'and I will show Vasudha to her room.'

When they were in the bedroom, Rohini sat down and said, 'Do you know what I have come to realise after all these years and all my foolishness? It is not what I did that I regret but what I did not do.'

'I am a married woman,' said Vasudha.

'Yes.'

'I wish that were undone. I wish I had not allowed my father to push me into this marriage. But I cannot bring myself to regret it.'

'Children change everything. I can never regret Aarav. Not even when he causes me pain.'

'Does he?'

'Love brings pain with it.'

Vasudha nodded.

'You must see the sunset here,' Rohini said. 'It's beautiful. And these days every sunset reminds me that the clock is ticking and my time here is limited—whether I go tomorrow or ten years from now, life will be short. It always is. If I had one piece of advice I could give to the people I love it would be: don't waste any of it. It is precious, this odd thing called time. It is the same for the king and the beggar, the industrialist and the worker. No one gets much more than is his due.'

'Are you lecturing her, Maa?'

It was Aarav at the door.

'Lecturing? Persuading might be a better word.'

'Leave that to me,' Aarav said with a smile but his eyes were serious.

'If you promise me results,' said Rohini, and for a moment Vasudha could see the family resemblance.

Aarav laughed. 'If only it were that simple.'

'If she were that simple, would she be worth seeking?'

'Those are fine words, Maa. Now I need to take her to Jeevan Uncle.'

'I will take her,' said Rohini.

They walked down a long corridor together, one that ended in an odd door. It could have belonged in a dispensary or a clinic. Behind it a nurse sat, reading the newspaper. She put it down and stood up and offered them both some hand-sanitizer.

'We need to protect against infection,' she said with the mechanical brightness of the efficient nurse. Then she took them into the next room where a thin figure lay in a bed, covered with a white sheet. His chest rose and fell as the life-support machine forced air into them.

'Jeevan,' said Rohini. 'The love of my life. I met him when Aarav was a baby and I was in no position to work. He took me in and offered me love. More than that, he offered Aarav love when he needed it most. And so he won my bruised and broken heart. What he wanted more than anything was to be a writer but it seemed that what he wrote found no favour. The manuscripts were always returned…when they were returned. Sometimes the publishers did not even send them back. That broke something inside him and he began to drink.'

She went and sat by Jeevan's side.

'Has Aarav told you…?'

'About his suicide attempt? Yes,' said Vasudha.

'It was his noble gesture. He did not want to be a burden on us any longer. So here is my last lesson for you. This is what happens to those who decide to make of their lives, a gesture. We only hear of those who succeed. We never hear of the failures, the gestures that backfire. This one backfired.'

Rohini remembered the long vigil at the hospital. Jeevan was in a coma but the public hospital to which he had been perforce admitted had given up on him.

'They told us to take him home and let him die but I was adamant. I don't know why I did it. I would not do it again nor would I ever tell a mother to put such a burden on her son. But I turned to Aarav and I said to myself, he will do this. He will pay for this. He will make sure that the next bottle of saline is not free. And my son, he ran out of the hospital and came back with some money. Then more. And more.'

When Jeevan stabilised they took him home and Aarav began to work.

'What did he do?'

'God forgive me,' Rohini said and there was a sob running under her voice, 'but I do not know. I did not ask. I only took. I was too wrapped up in Jeevan and when I turned around again, when I had a moment for my son, I found that he was a man.'

Vasudha felt her eyes fill. What was it about women, she wondered, that a man could fill their vision to the extent that they could see nothing else? Byron had put it well: 'Man's *love* is of man's life *a thing apart,* 'Tis woman's whole existence.' When she had read that in college, she had wondered what it must feel like to be so deeply in love. Hari had only wanted her body; he had no interest in her thoughts or dreams. Her soul was untouched even as he ravaged her body. But now that she had Aarav, now that she had fallen in love, what would she not give to be rid of this sweet torment?

Over the time they had spent in the car, she had become acutely aware of his person, the strength of his hands, the fine hair glowing in the sunlight, the quiet rumble of his voice.

Then he was in the room with her and Jeevan and Rohini and she felt a charge in the air again, the charge of her longing. Rohini stroked Jeevan's forehead with a gentle hand and then she looked at Vasudha.

'You have probably lived, as I did, with the notion of one man and one woman and one marriage that lasts for seven lifetimes. No man is brought up that way in India. But this is not a debate about feminism. I don't even seek to change your mind about marriage. But you should understand this—a true marriage is not created by a piece of paper or by a priest or by families and elders. It is created by a man and a woman. It is not to a sacrament that can be defined. It must be invented again and again because each successful marriage makes it anew and each failed marriage destroys it again. It is a huge challenge: to have and to hold, to be a man's ardhangini and share in his joys and sorrows and to know his heart, to accept him and to be accepted by him.'

Then she laughed suddenly and said, 'This is my family, such as it is. This is my son, such as he is. If you accept him, you should know that he will protect you with his life and his honour, with his heart and his body. If you take him, he will take you and keep you safe in his heart. I do not know if you will get a good bargain but then I do not even know if you will be a good bargain for him. But I have always, first and foremost, placed my trust in love. And this I can feel, I can sense, lives between you.'

~

The night was ripe with the scent of parijat. It always made her nervous, this flower. Its scent was delicate but it also had a touch of the other world. It was named for the magical wishing tree that came out of the churning of the ocean, the amrita manthan; and it seemed as if this was what was going on in her soul. A great rope was looping through her and as it writhed and shivered, the sea bubbled and frothed. What would come to the surface now? What was she called to do? How was she called to live? To what did she owe her allegiance?

She did not know when she got up and walked to the door but her stride was firm and decisive. It was as if a resolution had happened, catalysed by moonlight and parijata and the touch of cool cotton against her skin. She went to his room, again her steps lead by something that seemed outside her. That silly cliché now seemed real: this is bigger than both of us. It was.

In his room, she caught a whiff of him. It was his body, his essence, adrift in the room. But when she bent over him, his face, wiped clean of everything, had the gentleness of the little boy standing outside a sleazy nightclub and watching his world fall apart.

'But he is a child,' she thought. Somehow, becoming a parent forced upon one a maturity...

She turned from the bed and felt his hand reach for her sari and hold its pallu for a moment. She turned and his eyes were blazing in the night. There was male triumph in his eyes but when his hands found her body, they treated her with the care of a gardener treating a seedling.

~

They had breakfast quite late. Aarav was full of plans.

'We will fly to Bombay right now. The divorce papers will be ready. The grounds are clear. Desertion has been held to be clear grounds for divorce. And we have Mrunmalini Randive standing by. She's the best lawyer there is. I will, of course, take legal guardianship of Saanjh…'

'Slow down, Aarav,' said Rohini. 'Saanjh may be a child but he will also have some say in the matter. You must meet him and see what he thinks of you.'

'What he thinks of me…' Aarav began.

'Remember it has been only his mother and him against the world,' said Rohini.

'Sounds familiar,' said Aarav.

'I don't think you remember how you were with Jeevan when I first came home with him.'

Aarav looked uncomfortable.

'Well, yes, but I'm planning to marry Vasudha when her divorce is made final.'

'Is that better? Or worse? From Saanjh's point of view, I mean?' Rohini asked.

Aarav smiled.

'My reality check. Okay, we'll play it your way.'

'Not my way, beta,' said Rohini gently. 'The right way. The way of water.'

'So we go to Singapore first...'

'I don't have a Singapore visa,' said Vasudha.

'Then the mountain must come to us.'

And so it was arranged that Saanjh would fly into Madras and come to see them at the Retreat before they went to Bombay. Aarav also ordered an iPad.

'You shouldn't be trying to bribe him,' said Rohini.

'I'm not,' said Aarav. 'I'm just using whatever advantages I've got. You've got to be strategic about this.'

Vasudha realised with a little start of pleasure in her heart that he was nervous.

'I think it might be best to tell him about my guardianship a little later,' he said.

~

He wanted to win Saanjh's approval. But when the boy arrived, he stayed out of the way, allowing Vasudha time with her son. It was only when he was leaving that Saanjh got his iPad.

'Why now?' Rohini asked.

'I don't think he'd have paid his mother much attention if I'd given it to him when he arrived,' said Aarav.

'Don't be silly. That's his Mum you're talking about.'

Aarav smiled. He knew what young people were like when they were confronted with technology. He invested in many games companies and software development companies and they would all one day pay rich dividends.

In the car to the airport, Vasudha was content to play

second fiddle. It seemed as if everything might actually be all right now. A low moon floated alongside the car. Saanjh played with his new toy but he rested his small body against hers, seeking her warmth and her reassurance.

TEN

The air was warm and moist and smelled of the city: drying Bombay ducks and petrol fumes and sewage. It was the smell of a city that didn't really care too much for appearances. It was a challenge.

Vasudha stiffened her spine as she exited the aeroplane.

'We should go to...' Aarav began.

'No,' she said quietly. 'I have to go back alone. I will meet you at the hotel in two hours.'

'Let me drop you,' he said.

'I want to go on my own,' she said. 'I need to do this by myself.'

He nodded but it was clear that he did not understand.

Vasudha knew that she needed some time away from the spell of his presence. She needed to know what she was doing and whether it felt right at some fundamental level. She would only be able to find out when she was away from him. For, while he was there, nothing seemed impossible, nothing seemed un-do-able and nothing seemed wrong.

The taxi seemed almost improbably old now, after the cars of Dubai and the luxury of Aarav's modes of transport. But there was also a familiarity about it and she was happy that she found herself at ease inside it. I haven't lost touch with who I am, she thought. I like luxury but I do not need it. I must remember that. I must always remember that.

Outside the flat, Anil and Samson hovered and laughed and slapped each other but there was no sting to their remarks. Then she opened the door and stepped in, and she recognised that something was wrong. She felt it in the air. It was a familiar smell, not a welcome one, no, it was…

Hari!

And even as she identified him, his arm was around her neck, his harsh breath behind her ear sending tremors of disgust down her spine. Why had her father married her to this man who always made her feel as if a lizard had run over her body? A million questions tumbled through her mind. Where had he been? Why was he back? Why could she smell death? For a moment her blood ran cold and then she remembered that Saanjh was in Singapore, far away, safe. Her body sagged, as if in relief.

'Remember me?'

How could she forget? How could she forget the pain? How could she forget the torment?

'Yes,' she said. 'Hari.'

'Taken to saying my name now? What happened to the woman who wouldn't even say my name out loud.'

But he did let her go. He did not have much strength left she realised, as he slumped into a chair. His arms and legs were covered with lacerations and bruises. The smell of blood rose from them, iron-blunt but oddly organic as well.

'Sit down,' she said automatically. 'Let me look at those.'

'I'm fine,' he growled but let her guide him to a chair. She went into the bathroom and found antiseptic and cotton. He was dozing where she had left him, worn out and alone.

Patil. She should call Patil. His number was on her phone. She slipped to the door.

'Where are you going?' he asked. He seemed to have an uncanny ability to tell when she was trying to elude him.

'To get you some food.'

'Cook some. Now.'

'Don't be silly. There are no provisions in the house.'

She managed to keep her tone so matter of fact that he slumped back.

'Saambhar,' he mumbled. 'All those years, I could still taste your saambhar.'

She took a deep breath of the air outside. It was incredible, she thought, how quickly things could change around. Just half an hour ago...

'Arrey, just the two of you in there?' It was Anil.

'Why not let us in, too?' Samson said. 'We'll make it a party! Jahaan chaar yaar mil jaayen...'

She hurried away and the phone began to ring in her bag. She looked at it; it was Aarav.

Aarav. He seemed to belong to another planet, an alternative reality. For a while, she too had belonged there but now she was back. Where she belonged. She tried to call Patil but his phone simply rang and rang. She wanted to laugh. The police were never there when you wanted them. But he would see her missed call...

She dawdled as she bought supplies but eventually she knew he would come to find her. And what she did not need was a scene in the middle of the street. Those generally ended with a beating when they got back home. And now, suddenly, her bile rose. Why had she taken it? Why had she let herself be treated in that way? Why had she put up with him?

The answer came when she returned to the house and found him nursing his wounds. She set down her stuff and went to tend to him, as if by a reflex. All her life she had operated on this reflex. A man in trouble and her reflex was to go to him. Her father had needed her to dance attendance on him. Then her husband. Saanjh next, but at least there she had had the excuse that he was a child. And when he was old enough, he had begun to help her, almost without being asked. Her eyes filled.

She opened the bottle of antiseptic and began to clean the bruises she could see. Hari felt the gentleness of her touch. A woman. After all these years. His woman. He reached for her and she reared away.

'Vasudha?' he said. 'Are you scared of me?'

She looked up at him, without words. Then she could

see that he needed an answer as much as she needed to tell him what she thought.

'Yes,' she said, trying to keep it simple.

'It's me, Hari, your husband.'

'Yes,' she said. 'But the police have another version of who you are. They call you Hari, the terrorist.'

'Me?'

It came out as such a squeak of outrage that there was no way Vasudha could believe that Hari had ever been involved in wrong-doing.

'Then tell me,' she said. 'Tell me what happened.'

And at exactly that point Aarav chose to call again. She looked at the phone and perhaps her face changed infinitesimally, for Hari caught it. She silenced the call and put the phone on silent too.

'Who is that?' he asked.

The time for deceptions was over.

'It is the man I love,' she said.

'Bitch,' he snarled, venom in his voice. 'You're a married woman.'

'And you're a married man. Did that ever occur to you when you beat me? You're a father. Did that ever occur to you when Saanjh went hungry? You left us after a year of marriage. You tattooed your name on me as if I were cattle. You beat me and broke my spirit. What marriage should I have held on to? What husband should I have fasted for? You never once wanted to know me, who I was, what I thought, how I saw the world. I would have loved to tell you but you were only interested in the pleasure you could derive from my body. And Hari—did it ever occur to you that I got no pleasure out of it? Did you care? Did you offer one gesture of tenderness?'

'That is what you got. Me. You got me. Your father came begging. We have no dowry to give. We have nothing. But we have a daughter. So you got me. You should be grateful…'

'Yes. I was put on sale like an animal. And you checked my teeth and my health and took me home to your stable. There I was supposed to be a thing, a comfort, a bedwarmer, a cook, a housemaid, anything you needed. I knew that and I accepted it. I would not even have known what it meant to be loved had you not abandoned us.'

'I did not abandon you. I had no choice.'

Out of the corner of her eye, she could see the dial of the phone light up. Patil was returning her call. She did not let her eyes leave Hari's as she drew the phone under her pallu and silenced it. Then she called Patil back and cut the call. She kept doing this as Hari began to tell her his story, again and again, hoping that Patil would get the hint.

'I did not choose to abandon you. I was taking those mad Americans, I told you about them. All of the time talking about the real India and how they wanted to see tribal villages and this and that. I said chalo, let us show them then the tribal villages. I kept trying to choose places where we could get back to the city in time for dinner so I could have a drink too but they kept saying no, this is not what we're looking for, we want something more. They are like that. Until they have shat under the stars, they don't think it is real. So one evening, I just kept on driving…'

'The drive was long but the end was in sight. The village was just what the Americans wanted. It was picturesque and it was poor. There were pot-bellied children and old women leaning against mud walls. The photographs they wanted were all there and there was even a local mad woman who was often possessed by the spirit of some goddess and for the price of two bottles of hooch she put up a good display and the young people took video films and discussed the possibility of reshooting certain segments against another backdrop and getting her some vibrant clothes for effect.

They had decided to camp out under the stars when the Maoists came.' They rolled the Americans up, Hari said, sleeping bags and all.

'They might have let me go but by bad luck when one of them came and unwrapped my blanket, his face also came unwrapped. So I had seen his face and might identify him. I told him it was late in the night, that was what I would say, no one would know…But he didn't listen. He said, "We'll take no chances, boss. The reward on my head is big enough for anyone to be tempted, and you we don't even know. Just your luck." He was no ordinary Maoist, he was some big leader of theirs. So I was also taken as a hostage.'

Hari seemed to be taking some pride in his role in the whole thing.

What followed, he went on, was a nightmare of incarceration in various situations. Sometimes it was a simple jail cell and sometimes it was long forced marches. Sometimes the Maoists made him work for his supper, cleaning and cooking and washing their clothes and doing whatever odd jobs they could find for him.

And then came the flood.

They were all forced into the ashram of Father Peter Dayal. The good priest had worked in Orissa for decades and was suddenly confronted by a bunch of gun-toting men.

'I saw he was a good man and I told him what had happened to me. He told me that he would try to help me, but I had a better plan. The ashram was up on a hill but on the other side, there was a river. As the river rose, I realised that it was one way I could escape. So I found a big log of wood and I clung to it and pushed it over the side of the cliff and clung to it all the way down. Thank God it did not land on me but then suddenly I was in the water and being dragged along. Eventually I managed to get out and here I am.'

He had barely finished when the police burst into the room.

Hari was dragged away, protesting, and screaming abuse at Vasudha.

ELEVEN

Vasudha was true to her word. She was back in the hotel at the appointed hour. One look at her face, however, turned the mood sombre in the room.

'Hari. He's back,' she said.

'That might even make things easier,' said Apoorva. 'He sounds like a man who has a price…'

'He's been arrested.'

'Better and better,' said Apoorva. 'I think the courts might understand and expedite the case.'

But Vasudha was not looking at him. Nor was she hearing him. She was looking at Aarav. There were no words but it was as if a series of messages were passing between them, messages of despair.

'He's innocent,' she said.

And there was a dead silence in the room.

'You must free him,' she added.

~

Inspector Patil studied the man in front of him. After years of working with criminals, he could tell one when he saw one. He knew the kind of man who might kill or take a hostage or loot a bank. They were all very different from each other. But here in front of him was no criminal. He was an ugly customer all right, the kind of person who might hurt a woman or torment a dog simply because he could. But he was unable to think up careful and daring plans, much less execute them. He was a blubbering mass of despair at being in a police station. He expected the third degree and was already behaving as if it had been administered.

Then the phone rang on his desk.

'I thought I told you I did not want to be disturbed,' he snapped.

'Home Ministry,' said the sepulchral voice on the other side.

Inspector Patil sighed. He took the call. It was the home minister, a wily man called Shrikant Deshmukh.

'You have arrested a man in that Bastar hostage case, na?'

'Yes, sir but…'

'Patil, I am looking at your file. You are a man full of buts. You take your career seriously but this man is a find. The election is coming close and we need some closure on this case. Get him into court and get him to hang.'

'Sir, I don't think…'

'Do you know how bad it looked when that American

boy's body was found? Do you know how bad it is for our image abroad? Do you know how much tourism has suffered? Do you know how much work international relations takes? What you think is nothing against what you do not know.'

'Sir.'

'So let me tell you this. The public is a monster. It wants blood. It loves blood. It likes to read about blood. But it also wants blood spilled for blood spilled. This man will hang.'

The phone went dead.

Inspector Patil looked at Hari now with something like pity.

'You had better tell me the truth. Your life is seriously screwed up. Your wife is now with one of the richest men in the world. Your son is in Singapore. You had better tell the truth.'

'The truth?'

Hari's mind began to work, a rat in a trap. He knew what the Mumbai police were capable of. And the look on Vasudha's face came back. Yes, there was a way, he could make this all work. He could be assured of a good life in jail. He had only to avoid the truth. And then he might even win Vasudha back. She may want a life without him, but she wouldn't have it.

It was a desperate gamble, a gamble with his life, but it was one he was willing to take.

'Sir, I want to confess,' he said. 'I want to confess to the murder of Chad Tomkins and Cora Van Pelt, two American tourists whom I kidnapped in Bastar.'

Inspector Patil frowned at him but the Home Minister's voice rang clear in his ears. He said, 'In a case like this, I am leaving nothing to chance. I will have a magistrate here to certify that you have not been tortured or that this is not a forced confession. We will do this tomorrow.' Then he turned to an inspector and said, 'Get me the Home Minister.'

~

Vasudha, Aarav and Apoorva were sitting in the antechamber of Shrikant Deshmukh's office, but not for long. The Minister himself arrived at the door and opened it and ushered them in. Aarav Ruparel represented an investment potential that he would like to claim he had secured for the party and for the state.

'What may I do for you Mr Ruparel?' he began.

'You have arrested a Hari Prasad in a Maoist case.'

'Yes, indeed. Good work by our police force there. Second only to Scotland Yard, you know.'

'My husband is innocent.'

'You are?'

'Mrs Vasudha Prasad.'

'His wife,' Apoorva added.

'Pleased to meet you. It is perhaps the duty of every wife to say that her husband is innocent.'

'No. I wouldn't say it unless I knew it to be true,' Vasudha said, looking the Home Minister in the eye.

'But the courts will not believe you. They will believe him.'

'Believe him?'

'Yes. I just got off the phone with Inspector Patil. He said that Hari Prasad is willing to confess.'

'Confess?'

'What can we do? In order to make sure that there is no torture or conversation…'

'Coercion,' said Apoorva. The Minister frowned for a moment.

'Yes, that. So a magistrate is coming to see him and make sure he is all right. And once he confesses, he's on his way to the hangman. And nothing you can do or I can do will save him.'

They rose to leave.

'My advice to you is to get on with your lives. This is not anything you can handle, Mr Ruparel, not even with your money.'

Outside, in the car, Apoorva said: 'I don't get it. He's guilty. He's confessed. He goes to the hangman. You go to the wedding mandap. What about this seems wrong?'

Vasudha sighed. How could she explain?

'There's only one thing wrong. He's not guilty,' Aarav said, looking out of the window.

'And you know this because?'

'Vasudha says so.'

Vasudha looked at him. It was a look of gratitude. But something more. She wished they were alone, so that she could put her head on his shoulder and cry. It was as if she had been gutted.

'Come back with me,' Aarav said sotto voce, still looking out. A man stood in the middle of the road, shouting something to the heavens, while traffic swerved and weaved smoothly around him. 'You can spend the night at the hotel. In your own room.'

'No, I want to meet Hari.'

'I don't know how wise that would be.'

'I want to know why he has confessed to a crime he did not commit.'

Her phone rang. Patil was calling.

'Yes?'

Patil was brief. He wanted to talk to Aarav. She handed her phone over without a word. Aarav put it on speaker.

'Something is very wrong here,' said Patil. 'An innocent man is going to be condemned for a crime he did not commit.'

Aarav raised his eyebrows.

'But why is he doing this?'

'It's simple really. He has promised himself that he will go to the gallows so that his wife will be freed of him and will be allowed to marry you.'

Vasudha closed her eyes. She saw what Hari was doing clearly. From a position of no power at all, he was turning himself into a puppet-master. He was going to order her life from a jail cell. He was going to turn her into a fighter for him. And in so doing, he was going to get Aarav into his corner too. He would make them fight for him. He would make them go into war against their own dreams.

When Aarav put down the phone, his face was ashen. Vasudha understood. He knew what he had to do. He had to give her up and only then he would get her.

'Who's the best lawyer for this kind of thing?'

Apoorva looked up. 'I've sent out an APB to our legal departments. They've all come up with the same name: Robin Salve.'

TWELVE

All night she dreamed of flowers that unfurled to reveal skulls in their hearts. In the morning, Aarav greeted her at breakfast with hollow eyes. He had just gotten off the phone with his mother.

'Why does this always happen to me?' he had asked her.

'It doesn't always happen to you,' her answer was short and brutal. 'It happens to all of us.'

'I love her, Maa.'

'And I love a man who has not stirred from his bed for years. Every half an hour he must be turned over so that he won't get bed sores. Every hour he must be sat up and held up for ten minutes to let the water in his lungs move downwards. My love has had to live with all this.'

'I know, Maa.'

'So think of this. What is your duty now?'

'I don't know.'

'Your duty is to do that which makes your loved one happy.'

'Happy?'

'Aarav, my child, happiness isn't the word, I know. But this is what she must have—that man's freedom, or her life is blighted. Sometimes our happiness lies in squalid places. She has no choice. Don't make her beg.'

'Okay, so let's call it happiness, Maa. And making her happy means saving my rival.'

'Then that is what you must do and I expect you to do it with all the energy you once brought to saving the man I loved, and to building your empire.'

And so as he put down the phone, Aarav found that the only way out of despair was once again work. Once again, he was going into battle.

~

Apoorva arrived with an air of someone trying to bring good news to a funeral.

'The papers from Sujoy Bose. Signed, sealed and delivered.'

A line came back to Aarav from some long-forgotten class in religion: 'For what shall it profit a man, if he shall gain the whole world, and lose his own soul?' The world, it seemed, was his. But he had lost his soul's single desire.

He picked up the contracts and tore them in half.

'Give him back his damned hotel,' he said bleakly.

'What?' Apoorva was horrified.

'You heard me. Get it done. And let's go meet this Salve.'

~

Salve was an intense man with a brooding countenance. He listened to what Vaudha had to say and when she was finished, he made her repeat several aspects of her story again and again. Then he smiled in a slightly twisted manner and said, 'Father Peter Dayal.'

'Sorry?' Apoorva said.

'Father Peter Dayal. If Hari's story is true, this man can corroborate it. He can prove that the man is lying. And no court will accept a confession that is based on a lie.'

'Then we must go back to Bastar?' Apoorva asked.

'Indeed,' said Salve. 'Only we had better make it quick. They won't want to hang about waiting for this one. They'll want him hanging as quickly as possible.'

He turned and flipped on the television behind him. News channel after news channel had headlined the same news. Hari Prasad to die? Hari Prasad, the face of evil? Hari Prasad, the end of the road? People all over the nation were writing in, asking that he be hanged.

'No,' cried Vasudha. Then she looked quickly at Aarav. It was not horror at the thought of Hari dead. It was horror at the thought that her happiness should be based on the death of another. What kind of marriage would that be? One look at Aarav and her heart broke in several pieces. He understood. He knew what she meant. But she could also see the desolate look of a man who has had what he holds most precious taken from him. She saw a man who had no hope left. She wanted to reach out to him but there was no way she could do this.

She tried to send him her thoughts: 'I love you and I want you and I need you but we can never be together, not while Hari is alive and never if Hari dies. His corpse will dangle over our married bed forever.'

She would have given her life for a quiet moment in which to tell him this. No, she thought, I cannot give my life for anything. No parent has ever been able to give up her life as long as her children need her. I will have to live for Saanjh—but, my love, how can I tell you that there are things worth living for? Will you understand? Forgive me for this knowledge I have that I will find a way to live without you...

Aarav turned to Apoorva.

'You will make the arrangements?'

'Charter flight to Raipur booked. Takes off in two hours, clearance expected. Helicopter to Jagadpura booked and waiting. Father Peter Dayal will be expecting us.'

'Thanks, buddy. If anything happens to me, you know where things are.'

'Happen to you? What are you talking about?'

'I've signed the papers to make Saanjh my heir. I've willed everything to him. And there are trusts for Maa and for Vasudha. You get ten per cent of everything I own. Don't say no. It's worth a lot. It's worth nothing. I have discovered both these things. Take what the world gives you, my friend, as a gift. But use it as if it means nothing and watch as it multiplies.'

Then he was striding out of the room and Vasudha was

following him. Salve rose and said, 'This is not a case I'm going to forget easily.'

'It's not a day any of us is going to forget either,' Apoorva said softly.

~

Just before he left for the airport, Vasudha tried to catch Aarav's eye.

'Why are you doing this?'

He smiled. 'I have you to thank. You gave a homeless man a home in your heart.'

'You will always live there.'

'Then what more can I ask for?'

She saw that there was no turning back now. Not for him and not for her.

'I'll go and talk to Hari,' she said.

'No,' he replied. 'It won't be any use.'

She knew he was right, and looked at him in silent despair.

'I'll bring you back some mahua flowers, for our garden,' he said to her, smiling again. 'And you'll know where to find me when you want me, don't you?'

'Inside my heart,' she said to him, and it was a promise and a prayer.

~

In the end, it was simple. Father Peter Dayal was a man of god and there was nothing they had to do in order to get him to tell the truth. He spoke clearly and simply about Hari Prasad and how he had been brought to the ashram as a hostage. He said that the man was clearly not a Maoist, not a terrorist, but just collateral damage.

'Then why is he insisting that he's guilty?' asked Robin Salve, taking on the role of the criminal lawyer, even here in the simple precincts of the ashram.

'I can only say that he must have his own reasons. And these he will have to answer to his conscience and to God,' said the priest.

'But why would anyone want to take on the blame for something he did not do?'

The priest smiled quietly and looked at the crucifix on the wall.

'Is that so difficult to understand? We have had precedents before where the blameless have taken on the sins of others. We have had some do it out of love and there will also be others who will do it for motives that are much baser. Hari will have to decide where his motives lie.'

Apoorva hit 'save' and 'send'. The video clip went out to all the major channels. None of them would ignore it. The Ruparel Group was far too big an advertiser and Hari Prasad was far too big a story for them to miss the smallest detail.

It was done.

'I would like to take a walk,' said Aarav.

'Surely, my friend,' Father Peter said gently. 'But be sure you do not cross the barbed wire lines. Beyond that lie landmines. You step on one and you set it off. When you step off again, it will blow you apart.'

Apoorva walked with Aarav. He could see his friend's face was wiped free of care, as if some internal decision had been made.

'You're almost…'

Aarav looked questioningly at him.

'I don't know…happy?'

Aarav smiled. He put his hand on his friend's shoulder.

'I think every man has a mission, Apu. For some it's a long life. For some a meaningful life. I wonder whether we are given the choice. Whether we are asked, when in the spirit form, "What would you like to do—to leave a mark or to live out your days in obscurity?"'

'Well, if we are asked that, I probably chose obscurity,' said Apoorva. 'It was on your coattails that I got here.'

'We've come a long way together, friend. But now I need some time alone.'

Later, Apoorva was to say again and again that it was no unusual request. When a milestone had been passed, when something had been achieved, or a battle temporarily lost, Aarav would often go for a long walk on his own, as if to think things through in the quiet.

It was almost an hour later that he looked up from his iPad where he was following the tamasha that had ensued after the news channels aired the clip. The same people who were baying for Hari's blood now wanted him out. They wanted an investigation. The American parents of the young man had been contacted and were saying that they would fly down if need be to make sure the real culprits were brought to book. Minister Deshmukh was trying to keep his cool and a barrier of 'No comments' and 'We are looking into the matter'. And then Hari came into focus, coming out of jail.

'Aarav, you got to see this. She can divorce him on the basis of insanity, I'm sure,' Apoorva muttered to himself.

He looked out of the car just in time to see Aarav walk past the barbed wire and into the minefield. He knew he must have screamed his friend's name. He knew he dropped his iPad and crushed it as he stepped over it, running desperately to stop what he knew in his heart was inevitable.

Aarav turned one last time and offered his friend a smile of incredible sweetness.

Then the mine went off and threw Apoorva to the ground.

In two separate pooja ghars, the two women who were at prayer for a resolution knew almost to the instant when Aarav died.

EPILOGUE

The nurse didn't particularly like her duties but she did them with as much good grace as she could muster. Hari Prasad was not the kind of patient you wanted to deal with. She had been warned in the nursing school in Kottayam that the psychiatric ward was always a disturbing place and nurses burned out soon enough. But in a week she would be flying to Dubai and this would be behind her. She was going to be a plastic surgeon's nurse and it should be easy compared to this.

'Vasudha?' Hari asked as he always asked when she came in.

'No Vasudha,' said the nurse. 'Sister Lijjy.'

'Whose sister are you?'

'Every sick person's sister.'

'Then you cannot be my sister because I am not sick.'

'You take these pills and you will be well.'

'I will not take pills. They make me feel like I am half myself.'

'Being half-half will make you better,' she said.

'How long will I have to take them?'

She wanted to say: You have been taking these pills for twenty years now, ever since your breakdown and your release from prison. But she forbore.

'Why think about past? Past is past. Present you have. Future you may be better. So think about present and future and take your pills,' she said.

'Where is Vasudha?'

She wanted to say, 'In my pocket,' but once she had said that to an old lady asking after her son and the old lady had lunged at her with surprising swiftness and with even more surprising strength had ripped the pocket off her uniform.

'I don't know.'

'Who knows?'

It was a litany that never ended. Hari lay in his bed, drugged, shocked, fed, clothed, cleaned and a shell of himself. When the moon waxed full, he was tied up because he would try and make attempts to get away.

When Sister Lijjy had finally got his pills down his throat by a mixture of coaxing and coercion, there was a knock on the door.

'It's Vasudha,' said Hari. 'She has come.'

And outside the door was a beautiful young woman, elegant, one of those international Indians whose accents were polished in Switzerland and who tried very hard not to find everything about India contemptible.

'Is this Hari Prasad?'

'Iss,' said Lijjy, taking in the clothes and promising herself that she would try and get some just like them when she got to Dubai.

'He's my father-in-law,' she said and went in and touched his feet.

'Who is it? Vasudha?'

A frown of distaste crossed the pretty face.

'I am Avni. I'm your son Saanjh's wife.'

'Saanjh? Where is he? Where is my son?'

'I've come to take you to him.'

'See? See? They have come to take me to Vasudha. I will get dressed. I must have a bath. I want some clothes. Bring me some clothes. You are my bahu. I get to tell you what to do. Get me some good clothes. I will shave also. Come on, come on.'

Avni gestured to Sister Lijjy. They stepped out into the corridor.

'Should I tell him his wife is dead?'

Sister Lijjy crossed herself and offered up the prayer for the dead. Then she said, 'Go slowly, slowly. How much shock he will take?'

In the car, Avni tried to tell Hari something of Vasudha's life, how she had visited Rohini regularly until Jeevan's death, how Rohini had followed Jeevan a few days after he had slipped away quietly one night, how Vasudha had opened a nursery and had worked with greening the city she had grown up in, planting flowers in unexpected places, and how suddenly, one day, she had taken out a red sweater and had slipped into it and gone off to Bastar, back to the minefield where Aarav had died, back to the place, as if she had been called there.

Hari didn't seem to be paying much attention. He was looking out of the window with the rapt attention of a child in a new landscape. Then he turned and said, 'She is dead?'

Avni sighed.

'Yes, she's dead.'

Hari sighed, deep, long.

'Even in death, she went to him,' he said.

Avni did not know what to say to that. It was as if, she thought suddenly, your life was running along happily enough and then you discover that just next to it, there's *Romeo and Juliet* playing itself out.

And Hari turned eyes that were suddenly remarkably sane on Avni.

'I want to do the last rites.'

Avni nodded. She thought to herself: whatever.

But when the car turned into the long winding drive and they descended, Saanjh was back with the ashes. He stood on the top step with the urn clutched to his chest, as if trying to shelter his mother from the world.

'That is how to love,' said Hari with a sob in his voice. 'I did not learn it until it was too late.'

Saanjh looked at his father with a measure of disgust.

'I thought I told you to just tell him and come back,' he said.

Avni looked at him and said, 'Then you should have gone yourself. I did what a human being would do for another human being. I brought him to see his wife one last time.'

Hari tried to take the urn from Saanjh, who moved it away. Hari tried to hug Saanjh but his son turned away.

'Don't try this,' said Saanjh. 'You can sleep here the night. Then you have to go back.'

'I won't go back,' said Hari.

'No?' Saanjh was cold. 'Then you can wander the streets and die the vagabond death you deserve.'

'Saanjh!' Avni was shocked.

'She uses your name? Vasudha never used my name.'

'I use his name,' she said. 'And I tell him when I think he's being a shit. He's being a shit now. You come on in and have a cup of tea.'

'Avni…'

She turned and looked at Saanjh and said, 'He's your father. And when you become a father, I have the feeling you will be a much better one, if you make some kind of peace with this man.'

'My father was Aarav Ruparel. I even took his name.'

Hari shook his head sadly.

'No,' said Avni. 'You never did get a chance to meet Aarav Ruparel, did you? So your mother and your father were both Vasudha. But you cannot erase the fact that this is your biological father and he's a part of your history.'

'Past is past. Present you have. Future…' said Hari.

'No,' said Avni. 'The past is only the past when we lay our ghosts and forgive. Otherwise we let the past poison the present and ruin the future.'

Saanjh sighed a little.

'I suppose I did marry you because you have an independent mind.'

'Oh right,' said Avni. 'That independent mind is what caught your eye when you saw me in the swimming pool.'

Saanjh smiled a little.

'Come on, then,' he said to his father. 'We should talk.'